A sharply observed 24-hour urban love story that follows Stephen Connolly—a character from Wood's bestselling novel *The Children*—through one of the worst days of his life.

On this stiflingly hot December day, Stephen has decided it's time to break up with his girlfriend Fiona. He's thirty-nine, aimless and unfulfilled, but without a clue how to make his life better. All he has are his instincts—and they may be his downfall.

As he makes his way through the pitiless city and the hours of a single day, Stephen must fend off his demanding family, endure another shift of his dead-end job at the zoo (and an excruciating workplace team-building event), face up to Fiona's aggressive ex-husband and the hysteria of a children's birthday party that goes terribly wrong.

As an ordinary day develops into an existential crisis, Stephen begins to understand—perhaps too late—that love is not a trap, and only he can free himself.

Hilarious, tender and heartbreaking, *Animal People* is a portrait of urban life, a meditation on the conflicted nature of human–animal relationships, and a masterpiece of storytelling.

The novel invites readers to question the way we think about animals: What makes an 'animal person'? What value do we, as a society, place on the lives of creatures? Do we brutalise our pets even as we love them? What's wrong with anthropomorphism anyway? Filled with challenging ideas and shocks of recognition and revelation, *Animal People* shows a writer of great depth and compassion at work.

Praise for *Animal People*

'This is a compelling and ultimately moving novel that cements Wood's place as one of the most intelligent and compassionate novelists in Australia.'

ANGELA MEYER, *The Age*

'Charlotte Wood is one of our finest and most chameleonic writers . . . Wood's novels are often uncomfortable explorations of Australian life: seemingly modest in their ambition, the narratives are profound in their emotional scope . . . This is a beautiful, resounding tale of an ordinary man flailing. It's superb storytelling.'

REBECCA STARFORD, *The Australian*

'*Animal People* is the arch, poignant and funny story of Stephen, a no-hoper whose life unravels before his eyes as he is powerless to stop it . . . As the novel builds towards its climax, Wood's writing, consistently inventive and tightly crafted, notches up the lyric register and keeps the suspense. A few pages out from the end, I groaned. No, it can't be over yet. When I finished, I wanted to start it all over again.

CLAIRE SCOBIE, *Sydney Morning Herald*

'. . . an empathy so profound that when I finished the novel, I sobbed into my pillow with the raw, impossible vulnerability that is "being human".'

CLARE STRAHAN, *Overland*

'Even tighter and more nuanced than Wood's highly acclaimed previous work; its theme is enhanced by a wealth of subtly animal-themed metaphors—wet-eyed children with star-fish lashes, a woman like a ruby-throated hummingbird—and its heart-tugging climax is unexpected, reassuring and deeply satisfying.'

KATHARINE ENGLAND, *Adelaide Advertiser*

'There is plenty of wry humour here, but it is anything but jaded. It is what we could all use: a fresh pair of eyes for looking at an ordinary world.'

ELEANOR LIMPRECHT, *Sunday Age*

'Charlotte Wood's *The Children* is among my favourite Australian novels: she's just so good at the dynamics of relationships and minute social observations that give worlds of information about the people and places she captures. Wood's writing reminds me of Helen Garner's, in that it's easy to read, but deceptively so: it's rich with ideas and absolutely distinctive in its voice . . . *Animal People* may centre on a pending break-up, but it's a romantic comedy of sorts, with some wonderful observational humour—particularly at the children's birthday party in the final third of the novel. Thoroughly recommended; it made me laugh and cry. What more could you ask for?

JO CASE, *Readings Monthly*

'Young Australian writer Charlotte Wood is a class act . . . Wood's style is all intelligent observation. She maintains a sympathy for her characters even when their world seems grubby and hopeless. She weaves startling, specific descriptions into a plot without ever stalling or sounding pretentious. I found her descriptions of older people and upset children particularly moving, capturing humanity at its best and worst. Wood's books are an intimately rendered portrait of contemporary Australia and, as such, prompt readers to think about some of this country's real issues.'

ANNA FORWARD, *Sunday Tasmanian*

'Wood is a supreme reader of people. She methodically pulls back layers of human behaviour to their most basic forms of some laugh-out-loud results.'

PATRICK BILLINGS, *Launceston Examiner*

'Wood's understanding of relationships and her ability to create characters that are recognisable but fresh are ever-present . . . Even the detail given to secondary characters is perfect and adds authenticity. Wood's sharp funny observations are flecked throughout and add moments of comfort even when Stephen's having a dog of a day.'

JAMES WEIR, *Courier Mail*

'I read *Animal People* in one weekend and for me it had the intense, sustained poetic focus I usually associate with short stories—and an ending that packed such a punch I was almost winded . . . There are many moments of truth and beauty in *Animal People*.'

JANE GLEESON-WHITE, AUTHOR OF *Double Entry*

'Wood having a gentle dig at anthropomorphism, her softly-softly style so subtle you only realise how clever the writing is when exhaling at story's end.'

Qantas Magazine

'This is a sharply observed and often very funny portrait of an alienated man trying to make sense of the world . . . the novel's playful sense of the absurd is never far from the surface and keeps a jaunty tone.'

CAROLINE BAUM, *Better Homes & Gardens*

'It is said that it's the element of psychology—of peering into someone's very soul—that separates literary fiction from genre stuff, and if that's true, then *Animal People* is literature with a capital L.'

South Coast Register

'Wood is a consummate observer of the human condition. She distils the dynamics of families and the interactions of daily life, and writes about them with honesty and restraint . . . You don't have to be a man to empathise with Stephen Connolly. His core dilemmas are universal. Wood frames them in a character whom it would be easy to dismiss in the hands of a lesser writer.'

MIRIAM ZOLIN, *Australian Book Review*

Praise for *The Children*

'. . . *The Children* is beautifully and tightly shaped around Geoff Connolly lying insensate, tied to a breathing machine. His family waits, attacking one another but also finding and creating surprising moments of tenderness . . . Wood . . . has the ability to evoke matters of life and death without straining for effect. Her prose is convincing and her images precise . . .'

DOROTHY JOHNSTON, *Sydney Morning Herald*

'The bringing-together of an atomised family for an occasion or crisis is a time-honoured narrative strategy in fiction and film, and Wood makes the most of its possibilities both for drama and for social commentary . . . The reunion of three childless adult siblings plus their mother and brother-in-law makes for some very astute observation of how that family dynamic plays out, and also for some rather grim comedy as the demons of childhood rivalry and dislike re-emerge as ferocious and illogical as they were the first time around.'

KERRYN GOLDSWORTHY, *The Age*

'Charlotte Wood's writing is haunting, building tension so subtly the action hits like an unexpected blow. Her characters are wounded and human, their dialogue profound without meaning to be. Simple and real, this is a beautifully heavy and affecting story that will linger in your mind long after you've read the last page.' **** Highly recommended.

ANABEL PANDIELLA, *Good Reading*

animal people

CHARLOTTE WOOD

ALLEN&UNWIN
SYDNEY • MELBOURNE • AUCKLAND • LONDON

This edition published in 2012
First published in 2011

  This project has been assisted by the Australian
government through the Australia Council, its arts
funding and advisory body.

Australian Government

Allen & Unwin
Sydney, Melbourne, Auckland, London

83 Alexander Street
Crows Nest NSW 2065
Australia
Phone: (61 2) 8425 0100
Email: info@allenandunwin.com
Web: www.allenandunwin.com

Cataloguing-in-Publication details are available
from the National Library of Australia
www.trove.nla.gov.au

ISBN 978 1 74331 184 4

p. xiii: quote from 'Portrait of a Lady' reproduced with kind permission of
Faber and Faber Limited from *Collected Poems 1909–1962* by TS Eliot.

Text design by Gayna Murphy
Set in 13.5/16 pt Mrs Eaves by Bookhouse, Sydney
Printed and bound in Australia by Pegasus Media & Logistics

30 29 28 27 26 25 24 23 22

For SEAN

And I must borrow every changing shape
To find expression . . . dance, dance
Like a dancing bear,
Cry like a parrot, chatter like an ape.

TS ELIOT, 'Portrait of a Lady'

Whereas in animals fear is a response to signal,
in men it is endemic.

JOHN BERGER, *Why Look at Animals?*

CHAPTER 1

Stephen stood naked in his living room. He shuffled through the mail on the table, laying this sorting of envelopes and catalogues over the sickly, complicated guilt that had greeted him on waking. It was too hot already, even at seven o'clock, even here in the dark house.

He looked again at the junk mail flyer. STOLEN: *Have you Seen our Ferret?*

It was the same as the poster sticky-taped to the telegraph pole between his house and the shopping centre. He had often seen the skinny owner walking the creature on a leash on his way to the centre. The man was tall and pale with a small, delicate face, a black felt trilby and a greasy grey ponytail hanging down his back. He always wore tight, faded black jeans and a leather jacket too small for him, riding high above his narrow hips and short in the sleeves, his long white wrists protruding. In one dangling hand the man held a thin leather leash, and at the end of it the ferret undulated, long and low. Sometimes the ferret clucked in a strange, high stutter as it wafted and rolled. When they reached the shopping centre, just before the automatic doors slid open, the man would bend himself in half, scoop up the ferret and slip it inside his shirt, before straightening and sloping off into the cavern of the Plaza. Each time Stephen saw this he imagined with revulsion the creature's horribly elastic body, its claws clicking against the man's studded belt buckle, its fluffed fur against his bony chest.

Why would anyone steal a ferret? But there were the words, handwritten in photocopied black felt pen. *Someone has Stolen our Pet Ferret 'ANGEL' we miss her Dearly and want Her Back 'Reward'.* A phone number, an email address and a patchily inked photograph of the ferret. Its peaky little face stared out at the camera.

Stephen thought again of the creature's fur against the man's chest, the fine filaments rising, breathable and dusty. His own eyes and throat itched, and he rubbed a spread hand upwards over his chest and neck.

In the shower, Stephen scrubbed himself hard all over with the loofah brush Fiona had left here on one of those early visits last year, when she'd got a babysitter to stay over in Longley Point with the girls. They'd eaten dinner at one of Norton's cheap Vietnamese restaurants, and then gone to a pub to hear a punk country and western band called Big Fat Country. There, full of new middle-aged lust, they drank beer and allowed their hands to roam over each other's bodies in the crowded, noisy dark.

Stephen could not afford to think of Fiona like this today, but the image came to him anyway from one of those nights, right here in the bathroom: holding her gently against the tiles, gripping her sturdy, muscular bum with both his hands, her urging breath in his ear, the steam.

No. Stephen drew back the shower curtain and tossed the loofah into the handbasin. But one last flicker of sensation came to him, her slippery skin and then in the bed afterwards, her cool, moist hands seizing his hair, the twisting sheets, and now he gave in, leaning with his forehead on the shining tiles, cupping and slicking himself soapily until he came.

He stood beneath the beating water, already defeated by the day ahead.

The phone rang as he passed through the living room. He lurched, dripping. At this hour it could only be Fiona or his mother. He waited a few rings, breathing evenly, before picking it up.

'Hello, love,' said Margaret in a bright, innocuous voice. 'I know it's early, I just wanted to catch you.' This last bit as if she understood he was busy, as if the call would be quick. Stephen knew it wouldn't.

He held a hand over his groin, surprised by his mother's voice into guilt about what he had just done. 'Hi Mum,' he said, businesslike. Fiona said she could always tell when he was speaking to his mother by the guarded tightness in his voice. But if he relaxed the call would never end; best to pre-empt with a sense of urgency.

He pictured his mother in Rundle, standing in the hallway with the cordless phone, peering furtively out through the narrow pane of yellow frosted glass next to the front door, as she always did while speaking on the telephone. Or gazing at the floor, pointing her toe at the points of flower petals on the carpet, one by one, in a circular, unconscious ritual as she spoke. After their father died Stephen and his sisters insisted Margaret get a cordless phone so she could have one by the bed. But she plugged the charging unit into the same place as the old phone by the front door, and when she answered it she stood by the hall table as she had always done, as if still tethered there by the telephone cord. The only time the handset moved from the hall table was when Stephen or Cathy came to visit for a weekend and left it between the cushions of the couch or on the kitchen bench. The next time it rang Margaret would have to trot blindly through the house, listening, until she found it.

'Now I've just been thinking about the *television*,' Margaret said, as if this were a new topic. Her voice was still carefully bright, but there was an anxious note in it that made Stephen close his eyes. Sometimes he had seen her preparing for difficult conversations by writing down what she had to say, nodding to herself, straightening her spine for courage before making the call. He felt a throb of guilt.

'Right,' he said. In the past few weeks they had had at least four conversations about the television Margaret had her eye on. The Panasonic Viera 46-inch full-HD Digital Plasma. She was aghast in the first call when, after five minutes of her describing it he'd said, 'Sounds good, Mum. Why don't you get it?'

'It's too *expensive!*' she'd cried.

'How much?'

Margaret said, as if he was trying to pull the wool over her eyes, 'I know how much it is, don't you worry about that. It's ridiculous.'

He sighed. 'It's your money, Mum. You should do what you want with it.'

'It's *your father's* money,' Margaret said crisply. 'Which is *your* money, and Cathy's, and Mandy's. I have no intention of frittering it away on *televisions.*' She sniffed. 'That's what I said to Robert.'

Robert Bryson-Chan was the salesman at the giant new Good Guys electronics warehouse that had opened out on the highway, on the outskirts of Rundle. Stephen by now knew the life story of Robert Bryson-Chan, because Margaret had told it to him several times. He knew all about the salesman's parents, his engineering degree, his wife, his mortgage savings plan. His bloody tropical fish.

Stephen heard Margaret riffling pages. He knew the notebook she would be using, the one with little black-and-white cows printed all over the cover. On its blue-lined pages Robert Bryson-Chan had written the features of the Panasonic Viera 46-inch Plasma. Robert Bryson-Chan was clearly a patient young man; as Stephen heard the pages turn he felt a collegiate warmth towards him, in the way that two people sharing a queue with a garrulous bore might exchange sympathetic glances.

Margaret began—again—to read this list aloud. 'Full HD—that's high-definition—Plasma Panel,' she recited. 'Viera Image Viewer with SD card slot.'

A new thought occurred to Stephen: if she did get the television he could have her old one. It was big. He pulled the towel up into a tight short dress around his ribs and said, 'Mum, I think you should get the television.'

'One thousand and twenty-four times seven hundred and sixty-eight resolution,' Margaret said, as if he had not spoken. Now she had made it over the first hurdle of his conversational reluctance she showed an iron determination to press on.

Stephen pressed a fingertip onto a tiny opalescent shard on the tabletop and inspected it. It was either a bit of fingernail or a grain of rice. Rice, he decided, pressing the grain to his front teeth and nibbling as his mother went on about standby power consumption and energy ratings. He pulled a thread of fluff from his tongue. The tabletop was greasy, it really needed a clean. He swapped the phone to his other hand and pulled the towel from his waist, began wiping the table with it.

He surveyed the whole living room then with new, post-Fiona eyes. Over the past year, as he spent more and more time at her place on the other side of the city, this had become less his home and more a storage unit for his things. His *old* things, he saw now. Like the couch, a curved blob of Ikea foam covered in dusty black quilted cotton. The other things were mostly cast-offs from his sisters or from garage sales: the small square dining table with the rippling blonde-wood veneer and the three flimsy folding chairs; the low, angular ornamental bookcase where a few Dostoyevsky and Brett Easton Ellis and Camus novels were stuffed in between phone directories and takeaway menus. A corner of one of the girls' texta drawings poked from between the menus. He bent to draw it out while his mother talked, the phone held between his neck and shoulder. He rubbed dust away from the corner of the page and smoothed it out on the tabletop. It was one of Larry's mobile phone drawings: the white page empty but for a small line, at the bottom of the page, of lumpen purple oblongs covered in emphatic dots, a crumpled little aerial worming up from each phone. He should throw it away. He should throw all this stuff away. He folded the paper in half and half again, and pushed it back between the books.

His mother's voice washed over him as he appraised the rest of his living room. There was the nest of swirly-caramel laminated occasional tables that even his sister Cathy had not wanted; the single monumental green armchair with its frayed maroon piping. A lamp or two would help. Although it would mean another set of extension cords, snaking around the skirting boards to the single power point, where an outcrop of double adaptors already bulged from the wall.

It was one of the things that made Fiona's place so spaciously adult: electrical cords and power points were all invisible, built into walls.

Fiona had stayed over here a few times early on, but only a few. It was soon obvious that her place was *the* place; her large house by the water had soft, lavish couches and a fridge full of proper food—vegetables, and two types of milk, and cooked chicken legs under plastic wrap. Stephen's fridge held a block of cracked yellow cheese, an ancient container of leftover takeaway, two six-packs of beer and, for some reason, a heavy jar of flour. Fiona's place was full of matching crockery, fruit in bowls, glassware, framed paintings. It was part of the problem: her house was a monument to a marriage, even if it was long over.

Of course, at Fiona's there were also the girls.

His chest tightened at the thought of Ella and Larry. They visited his place occasionally, all of them arriving—with him—as a team, to pick up mail or for some other errand, on the way to somewhere else. Their visits here had the air of an outing, like going to the zoo or some hokey, familiar museum. While he unlocked the front door the girls would flip the heavy lid of the letterbox and pat the faded cement gnome's head, and Fiona would idly deadhead the few strands of yellowing, woody basil that poked from the front-yard weeds. Once inside, the girls would pelt up the hallway, through the kitchen and out the back door to the toilet in its little shed at the end of the yard, sitting on the huge white throne of it with the door open, gripping the sides of the seat and peering out. Or, they would race to the mantelpiece of op-shop curiosities they loved: the cast-iron figurine Fiona called the Racist Moneybox—a bust of Ella Fitzgerald with whorls of bulging iron hair and big red lips and a cupped monkey-hand on a lever, which fed coins into her mouth when you pressed it—or the smelly little animal-skin drum Stephen's sister Mandy had sent him from Afghanistan. The girls fought over the big green chair, clambering to end up both squashed in it, shrugged up together against its vast back cushion, their feet only just reaching past the sagging seat.

When they left his house they left as a foursome; the visits were quick and cursory and after those first few lustful weeks he could not remember Fiona ever sitting down in his house.

He decided to be glad of it now, as he looked around. This was his place. After a good clean-up—he had not noticed before how filthy the windows were—he would be glad to be here again, have his life back. He tested the phrase cautiously in his mind—yeah, *got my own life back.* It would sound right in a few weeks. When he got used to it.

His mother was still talking, and it was almost half-past seven. He went to the bedroom, looking round for clothes. He had to get a birthday present at the shops for Ella and then hit the road. The working day loomed, shadowy and life-sapping, with the deep fryer to be cleaned, the bloody teambuilding event. After that, Ella's party. And then—he forced it past in one sharp swipe—telling Fiona.

'I have to get going, Mum,' he said, dragging underpants up one wet leg.

'The trouble is,' said Margaret, 'that the last time I went, because I wanted to check about the standby consumption, Robert wasn't there. It was his day off. There was just a girl with a pierced eyebrow, and *she* said the only thing really to be concerned about was inches for dollars.' She paused again, and when Stephen gave no reply she said, 'But I don't think that's right.'

He glanced out of his bedroom window. Beyond the council workers unloading gardening gear from a ute, the checkout operators from the supermarket had begun to arrive for work. Pretty Greek and Indian girls in their ugly green uniforms, getting out of large cars driven by their boyfriends. The older, rough-voiced Australian women trudged in from the car park. Stephen knew them all, or at least their faces, and they knew his. But they never acknowledged one another across the black rubber belts of the supermarket counters.

He extracted a t-shirt from the dirty laundry pile and held it to his face to smell, before tossing it on the bed, smoothing with one hand and scanning it for stains. Not too bad.

'Anyhow, what she *did* say was they have a special offer.' Margaret brandished this sentence, showing she did have something new to report. Before he could answer she said, with practised relish: 'A bonus Wii.'

'Mum, I have to get to work,' he said.

His mother sighed in exasperation. 'Do you know what a *Wii* is, Stephen?'

'Not really.'

'Well it's a game, that you play on the television, and you can get fit. I think it would be very good for me. The doctor said I need to exercise, especially now.' She sighed again. 'I sent you a *link* about it. Did you even get it? You never reply.'

'My computer's broken,' he lied, glancing at the dusty laptop propped open on the chest of drawers. He had not turned it on for months.

'What's wrong with it?' she demanded, suspicious. 'Mine's never had a problem.'

Margaret loved her laptop. At the kitchen table in Rundle she sat before the sleek black machine, a floral cloth on the table, the sun at her back. She would have unzipped it from the padded black computer backpack to which she religiously returned it whenever it was not in use. The optimistic tilt of her chin, the way she adjusted her glasses with her fingers up to her face like blinkers whenever she peered down the screen. All this—the packing and unpacking of the computer four times a day, the careful way she would read and make sure she understood every irritating menu that popped into life on the screen—was both poignant and exasperating. Stephen was unnerved by her growing command of technology.

Before his father died the old cement-coloured monitor and keyboard in his 'office'—Stephen's old bedroom—were foreign objects to Margaret. The computer was Geoff's particular shrine, untouched by Margaret except occasionally with a brush on the nozzle of the vacuum cleaner. It was as inanimate to her as a cricket bat, only coming alive when Geoff sat before it, stabbing at the keyboard with two fingers and scowling at the screen with the suppressed rage he felt whenever he didn't understand something.

But after he died, Stephen and his sisters bought their mother the laptop, and Cathy set her up with email and Skype accounts, and Margaret went to an

Introduction to the Internet course for Seniors at the local library. Where she was astonished to find that the use of technology came to her intuitively, with ease and pleasure. Now she sent Stephen emails by the dozen, and carried her mobile phone everywhere. She used acronyms in conversation—*Did you get my SMS? I sent you the URL!*—and appeared most of all to enjoy being part of a new era which had left her friends behind. Even the men, she would say smugly, could barely switch a computer on. If Stephen or Cathy visited Rundle their mother would insist on Skyping Mandy, who would wave at them from the screen and then weave her laptop around the room so they were transported—vertiginously, miraculously—into the hotel room in Kabul or Baghdad or Islamabad.

Cathy had told Stephen their mother was even thinking of starting a *blog*. It would be called Margaret's Musings, he supposed. Or Rundle Ruminations.

Down the phone line her voice took on a quick, sly tone: 'I could ask Robert about your laptop,' she said. 'You could bring it when you come, and he could have a look at it!'

Fuck.

Margaret was silent for a second. When Stephen did not reply she said evenly, 'You are coming next weekend, *and'*—adding this emphatically, as if saying would make it true—'bringing Fiona-and-the-children. You *are*, Stephen.' Warning, plaintive.

Stephen lay back across his bed. He stared at the ceiling. He had forgotten. This, not the television, was the reason for his mother's call. This was what lay beneath the planned brightness in her voice, the prattling on about Robert Bryson-Chan. It was a circuitous, duplicitous stroll, leading him into this ambush.

Next weekend would have been his father's birthday. And now, inexplicably, four years after Geoff's death, Margaret was giving a birthday party. For her dead husband, in Rundle. Mandy, of course, was out of the country (he sent out another spiral of resentment towards her for this), and so Cathy and her new boyfriend Dave, and Stephen and Fiona and the girls—whom Margaret had assiduously tried to fashion mentally into her own grandchildren, despite the fact they didn't know her name and wouldn't recognise her in a photograph—must be there.

It was months ago that Cathy bailed Stephen up about this. She had cornered him, and he had agreed. She made him promise. But everything had changed. Cathy didn't know; nobody but he knew that after today there wouldn't be any Fiona-and-the-girls to bring.

He felt a panicked flare of fury towards his mother. He could imagine the invitation list, the dwindling set of his mother's small-town friends boasting of their grandchildren and sons-and-daughters-in-law. He saw his mother's urgent logic: she must work quickly, this state of affairs could only last so long before Stephen ruined it by losing another girlfriend. He was In A Relationship—it was an endangered condition, must be captured, preserved.

But it was too late.

'We'll see, Mum,' he said, closing his eyes. 'I don't know though, actually. I don't know if we can make it after all.'

'Oh, Stephen!' Margaret cried. 'I *emailed* you, and *texted*, and you promised Cathy, you said you *would!*'

He didn't say anything. He heard her breathing.

'I don't think I have ever asked you for very much,' she said in a small voice.

Oh, there it was. A final push of mutiny rose in him. He stood and looked around for his shoes.

'I think you should buy the television,' he said flatly.

She was silent. Was she crying? He strained to listen. In the long moment of her silence he heard the disappointment he had always been to her, and the vain effort she had always made to hide it. His resolve faltered.

'I'll let you know,' he muttered. 'Fiona can't make it but I might be able to sort something out.'

She would know he was lying.

'Okay?' he said, more gently. More silence. Well, fuck her then. He said curtly, 'I have to go to work.'

Margaret spoke at last, haughty and wounded. 'Well. Thank you *very much*, Stephen.'

Sarcasm did not come naturally to her; her bald attempt at it clutched at him. He began to speak but Margaret interrupted, quite coldly now, that she had the tennis newsletter to do and—with emphasis—she didn't want to *hold him up*. She hung up.

Stephen punched the telephone handset into the bedclothes and lay back again, groaning *fuck* and *shit*. He hated this obnoxious need of his mother's for him to be improved, her years of cautious hinting that he could do better if he only tried. Her phases of sending him job advertisements cut out from the newspaper had evolved, of course, into sending him *links*.

'You've got a lovely mind,' she wrote in one email a year ago. 'We just wish you would use it.' We, as if she was still talking about his father. Who else was meant by *we*? It was insulting. He replied with four words. *I use my mind.*

But then, almost as soon as Stephen began seeing Fiona—even despite the strained familial complications—it seemed Margaret had decided this fact was achievement enough. She had adjusted her expectations of him so far downward over the years that even Fiona's children by another man could somehow be counted as an accomplishment of Stephen's. Margaret showed photographs of Ella and Larry to her friends—Stephen winced in shame and pity—as if they were her own grandchildren.

He sat up, and now turned his blame to Cathy. She had, without protest, accepted their mother's pretences about the stupid fucking party. She knew it was nothing to do with their father, that it was simply for Margaret to show off to her friends—and she had talked him into it too. Cathy probably *wanted* to parade her boyfriend in front of the geriatric Rundle crowd. She was as pathetic as their mother.

He dragged a shoe from beneath his bed with a hooked finger, filling with bitterness. Mothers were supposed to think you were magnificent no matter what. Sisters were supposed to side with you. But instead they kept grasping at him, making him feel guilty, expecting things of him he could not be expected to deliver.

A weariness rose in him as he realised his mother would straightaway call Cathy to complain. He could add another martyred, angry phone call, then, to the troubles that lay ahead. The acres of the day unrolled before him: all the different kinds of disappointment he would be, all the various arenas of his failure.

He turned away from the mirror, and stood to worm first one narrow foot, then another, into his trainers.

The sun was high, relentless in the clear sky as he slammed the door behind him and turned out of his gate. As he stepped from the shade of the house onto the footpath he was stunned motionless for a moment—Christ almighty!— by the white brilliance of the heat. He stood shielding his eyes with his hand—he would have to go back for a hat—when Nerida from up the road called out to him. He hesitated, looking down towards the Plaza. He wished he could pretend he hadn't seen her, but he was caught.

Neighbourliness made him uneasy. In Stephen's trudging back and forth to the outdoor toilet over the years he had developed almost without realising it an intricate sonic awareness of his neighbours' private lives: the wheedling voices they used to talk to pet cats and dogs and birds, their habits with power tools and garbage bin lids (droppers or lowerers). He knew which back doors had aluminium flyscreens and which were sliding glass, he knew whose water pipes banged and filled at strange hours in the night, and he knew who had sat in their courtyards illicitly smoking when their partners or children were in bed. Occasionally, on the night air, came the floating grunts of sex.

But this was backyard knowledge. In the street, at their front gates, Stephen and his neighbours maintained the barest of greetings and he imagined that, like him, they were happiest that way.

Except for Nerida.

Retired Nerida and her girlfriend Jill—he was sure they were gay, though never sure enough to venture any remark that might reveal this—lived two houses from Stephen, on the other side of Bridget and Keith, who had moved out with the new baby while the renovations were done. Today the builders were absent, the house silent.

From her gateway Nerida beckoned at him again with a box of snail pellets. Stephen moved down the pavement and into the shade cast by her verandah. This was necessary—the sun was unbearable—but regrettable, as she took his nearness as a signal that Stephen was waiting for confidences. She beamed, tilting her head towards Bridget and Keith's.

'Spending a lot of money in there,' she said, in a tone that meant fools and gold were soon parted.

'Right,' said Stephen. To keep out of the sun he had to lean towards her; it might look eager. He must make it clear he was in a hurry. 'What's up?' he said.

Nerida's face was square and masculine, like a nun's, her metallic grey hair swept back from her forehead. She wore short-sleeved floral blouses with the collars ironed flat—today's was maroon. The cobweb thread of a fine gold chain with a tiny crucifix lay against the sun-damaged skin of her chest.

Nerida said again, nodding at each word: 'A *lot*. Of money.' She still held the snail pellet box aloft. A cartoon snail grinned evilly from the box, showing its white human teeth, raising its villain's eyebrows. Strange, how poisons were so often labelled with pictures of the pest being schemingly wicked. Stephen supposed it would be harder to kill a snail if you thought it was innocent. If the box had instead, say, a picture of a snail writhing in slimy agony, vomiting blood. If snails had blood.

Nerida was waiting for him to respond, her free hand delving recreationally inside the roomy pocket of her trousers.

He said nothing; he did not want to allow Nerida the pleasure of telling him how much was *a lot*. She'd once uprooted three little native shrubs Stephen had planted on a whim in the nature strip, and replaced them with another two clumps of agapanthus. He hated agapanthus; they reminded him of Fiona's parents' long lawns on the far side of the city. But the agapanthus flourished, and the one grevillea Stephen guarded had neither grown a millimetre nor died since he planted it. It stood twenty centimetres high, atrophied in the shadow of the lush, healthy straps of the agapanthus leaves.

He saw Jill looking down at them from the verandah. The German shepherd, Balzac, was a shadow in the gloom of the hall behind her. Jill had never once, in all the time he had lived here, said hello or spoken to Stephen. Just as his glance met hers now, she averted her eyes as she always did, and stared down the street at the man from the Plaza starting up his leaf blower. Together they watched the leaf-blower man's slow, zigzagging pursuit of three different leaves. One by one, he escorted each leaf across the footpath into the gutter.

'I see the beggars have got at your place again,' called Nerida to Stephen over the noise. She meant the graffiti tags adorning his fence in the back lane. The fence was covered in the squiggles and swearwords and odd, mysterious expressions: *Hazfelt is Ace*, or *Carl Scully is a deadshit*. Or in one place, in small black felt pen: *forgive me*.

With those two words Fiona's wide, grey eyes last week—her light puzzlement as she asked him if anything was wrong—came into his mind. But he could not allow this scrutiny today, could not bear the steadiness of her gaze. It must be banished.

'I'll paint over it,' he said to Nerida.

Up on the porch Jill stooped to hook a leash to Balzac's collar. The dog was elderly and losing his sight, with a deep, loosely shaggy coat that to Stephen, with his dander allergy, was even more floatingly hairy than the fur of ordinary dogs. But as always, as soon as Balzac's cloudy old eyes made out Stephen he strained at the leash, pulling Jill along behind him down the stairs and out of the gate.

Stephen called, 'Hello Balzac,' in a weary manner that he hoped might convey to Nerida and Jill just how little he enjoyed what was to come next, and that might even (he knew this was futile) distract the dog. But there was no stopping Balzac doing what he always did—skirting round behind Stephen in a neat side-step, planting his brawny weight on the pavement and lodging his snout firmly up between Stephen's buttocks. 'Hellooo,' said Stephen, trying once again to laugh it off and skipping forward, wriggling to dislodge Balzac's nose. It made no difference, it never made any difference: the dog merely followed with his own heavy steps, nuzzling his broad snout a little further in. It felt to Stephen that he was balanced on the dog's nose, legs dangling.

Nerida and Jill gazed fondly down at the dog. 'He loves to say hello, don't you boy,' said Nerida. '*Donechoo,*' she repeated, in the low, guttural baby talk people used with dogs.

At the sound of Nerida's voice Balzac gave a shiver of enjoyment and, as always, Stephen was forced to reach down behind himself and push the dog's snout firmly down and out of his bum. He followed this with a swift half-turn, quickly positioning his backpack at his groin so Balzac couldn't begin again at the front.

Balzac licked his lips in a dejected way.

'Sorry,' Stephen called over the noise of the leaf blower, and then shouted his usual addendum: 'It's just that I'm allergic.' The skin of his fingers that had touched the firm, hairy planes of Balzac's snout began tingling with allergic activity. He felt an urgent compulsion to wash his hands.

Jill dropped into a crouch, pulling Balzac to her. She put a protective arm around the dog's broad, shaggy girth to shield him from Stephen's insulting allergy, and crooned apology into his ear: 'It's all right boy, it's okay.' She pushed her face close to the dog's, and closed her eyes. Balzac yawned wide, then extended his long elastic tongue and licked at Jill's offered mouth and nose and eyes with enthusiastic, probing strokes.

Stephen felt nauseous watching this drooling exploration. 'Sorry,' he said again, annoyed with himself for saying it. Behind his back he splayed the fingers of the hand that had touched Balzac's wet nose. He imagined the sticky paths made for the allergens running all up and down his hand. He pictured them: microscopic cartoonish creatures pricking at his skin with their sharp claws, waiting to spring into his eyes on their tiny chemical feet if his hand strayed to his face. Stephen knew this was silly, but his nose and eyes begin to itch and water anyway.

'Have you seen this?' Nerida said, nodding at the telegraph pole where a copy of the lost ferret flyer was sticky-taped. 'Isn't that revolting! What kind of a person would keep a *ferret!* Good riddance, I say.'

Jill murmured in appalled assent.

'But I suppose they feel like you would if you lost Balzac,' Stephen said. Jill and Nerida looked at him, then each other. 'I don't *think* so,' muttered Jill. It was the most direct thing she had ever said to him, but she still didn't look up. She pursed her lips and went back to letting Balzac lick her face, up and down, in long syrupy strokes, while Nerida peered at the ferret picture, shaking her head.

Something about her stance—that hand over her mouth—brought Stephen's mother to mind again. *I don't ask you for much.* Something else she said had set up a tinny alarm, faint but persistent, in the depths of his mind.

'I have to get to work,' he said to the women. He waved his keys and turned away towards the Plaza.

How anyone could let a dog lick their face, their mouth, was beyond Stephen. They could watch a dog happily licking its balls, or worse, and then—he felt sick again as he crossed the street, towards the centre's entrance. But Nerida and Jill were Dog People. They identified it early in any conversation with someone new. We are dog people. Are you a dog person?

Stephen knew he demonstrated some lack of humanity by not being a Dog Person. This seemed unfair. He was not a cat person either. He was not an animal person in the same way he was not a musical person, or an intellectual person. One was born to these things, like the colour of one's eyes, or the length of one's legs. Not to be musical or intellectual was unremarkable and provoked no suspicion. But not to be an animal person somehow meant he wasn't fully human.

When Stephen told people he worked at the zoo their faces would light up. 'Oh, I love animals! How wonderful!' they gushed. How lucky he was, how privileged. They held him in high regard, and waited for tales of giraffe-teeth cleaning or lion-cub nursing. When he told them he worked only in the fast-food kiosk, their faces fell. But then they recovered. Still, to be surrounded by all those beautiful creatures. He usually agreed at this point, to finish the conversation. He did not say he found the zoo depressing. It was not the cages so much as the people—their need to possess, their disappointment, the way they wanted the animals to notice them.

He supposed being an animal person meant you liked to caress animals, be licked by them. That you did not fear them, nor they you. They gave you *unconditional love*. What was this love? Was it like love between people? He felt this to be impossible, but animal people did not agree. Some claimed their dog's or cat's love was greater than human feeling. After Stephen's father died and he returned to the data entry place where he worked back then, a receptionist made sympathetic noises about his loss. 'I know just how you feel,' she said: her dog had died three months before. Stephen had tried to be offended, but found it hard to muster the energy. He could not understand it, but he believed her when she said his grief and hers were parallel. For she was an animal person. She believed her dog chose to love her, could recognise her as special, in the same way a father could love a son.

But Stephen was unnerved by them. He feared the hair of animals, its quivery ability to float towards him and stick to his skin. And then it would begin, as it was beginning now: the watering eyes, the congested nose, the desperate desire to wash himself down. The furious itching in the eyes, then the sides of his nose, forcing him to scratch and rake at his face till it was red. He would have to lean into a bathroom sink and rinse his eyes, but no matter how much he did this, the fierceness of the itching would not abate until he was far away from the creature, and had changed his clothes. Cats were the worst, but dogs too, horses, rabbits, anything with hair or fur. Worst of all was the way they insinuated themselves upon him. It was true, the little jokes people made about cats going to people who didn't like them. But it was not a joke. Though it would only make things worse, he screwed the heels of his palms into his eye sockets, twisting and gouging at the unbearable itch.

He made himself stop then, and tried to ignore the itch—don't *scratch*—along with the low humming anxiety about his mother, and the much more sombre, deeper chord, about Fiona.

At the Plaza entrance the small, tidy woman who sold the *Big Issue* magazine had already set up next to her camping chair. She wore her red vest and her baseball cap, her long, thick grey ponytail behind. And the man in the wheelchair was there again.

Stephen felt sorry for the *Big Issue* woman. She was about fifty, small and wiry, with a broad, husky voice that to Stephen evoked a life of hard knocks. She had gaps in her teeth, mostly remembered to keep her mouth shut when she smiled. She stood outside the Plaza every second day or so for hours. Stephen usually bought the magazine, but not always. A stack of unread *Big Issues* lay on the floor by his couch.

He sometimes wondered where the woman lived, whether she was really homeless. He couldn't imagine her living on the street—she looked healthy and well-kept, purposeful. Perhaps she was saving up to buy a house. He pondered now, nearing her, whether this was allowed. If you were very successful, at what point did the *Big Issue* people tell you that you weren't allowed to keep being a vendor? Once or twice he had pictured the woman in some grotty refuge in the inner city. He imagined she kept her area of a broken-windowed dormitory scrupulously clean, her bed always made, but he worried about her living in such a place, with the junkies and the violence and the filth. He worried about her being robbed, her *Big Issue* money taken from under her mattress while she slept. But this anxiety only visited him if he had bought a magazine, when he felt some responsibility for her well-being, and it only lasted for a moment. Mostly it was easy not to think of her at all. He had seen her occasionally in civvies buying cigarettes or groceries and looking, without her red vest and cap, like any other shopper. He felt an odd pride for her then. He once said this to Fiona, but she gave him a strange half-smile and said the woman *was* just like any other shopper.

He passed by them now, the woman and the wheelchair man. The wheelchair man was about thirty, and was often at the Plaza, whizzing along the wide aisles. Stephen had developed a deep dislike of him over the months, with his little crossed feet and his sparse, mousy beard and his thin grey jumpers. The man had a proprietorial air about the *Big Issue* woman. He always bought a magazine, and then she would have to stand with her awkward smile and listen while he talked at her, and they both knew that this, not the magazine, was what he had paid for. Often the man was still there, berating her, when Stephen came out of the Plaza an hour later; the woman would still be smiling, nodding wearily.

From the fluorescent interior of Jungle Jim's up ahead came the familiar funky stink of mouse shit and dog biscuits. Stephen had bought a goldfish there once. To him a goldfish seemed the ideal domestic creature. You could sit by and watch its graceful movements through the water. Just the fact of a fish pond, Stephen thought, lent a special Oriental peacefulness to the place. It was a golden thread linking him in his Norton backyard, despite the leaf blowers and the aircraft noise and the abandoned shopping trolleys, to the world's ancient wisdoms. A goldfish slid through the dark water, dignified, detached and silent, heedless of him.

Also, it was hairless.

But the goldfish had died. He learned later you were first supposed to do things to the water, but he hadn't known this, and over twenty-four hours the fish swam slower and slower in the water of the big cracked garden pot, and then developed a whitish desiccated coating, and finally floated horribly on its side. He had to scoop it out and bury it beside the old staggery lavender bush.

It came to Stephen suddenly that all his mother's friends were dying.

First his father, and now their friends, one by one. Every few months his mother had to stand in the Rundle graveyard and watch a friend lowered into the ground. He had never talked to her about this, and she had never mentioned it except in passing. But each time he went to Rundle he saw the growing pile of homemade funeral service booklets on the table by the phone.

The pet shop woman was sorting through the lumpy display of dog-chewing things as he glanced in through the door. A flash of revulsion went through Stephen at the sight of those strange bone-like objects, their seeped-on bandage colour. In the glass compartments of the window were three puppies on the upper level, and one lone guinea pig on the lower floor. The sign on the dogs' level—no matter what breed was in there—said '*Pomeranian Maltese X*' and '*Shi-tzu*' (Stephen remembered his boss Russell's worn joke about how the zoo had replaced the lions and elephants with one small dog: 'It's a shit zoo!') but the puppies all looked the same to Stephen. They leapt and yapped in their knee-high bed of shredded paper. A sign said DO NOT TAP ON THE GLASS and had some small print about RSPCA regulations against tapping on pet shop windows. Soon the sun would strike the glass directly and stay there all day until sinking below the Plaza roof peak in the afternoon. The puppies would stop leaping and lie panting in their white forest of shredded documents.

The guinea pig snuffled, a hairy caramel all-sort, forgotten in the far corner of the window.

Stephen's eyes still itched; he ran his hands down his jeans again to stop himself rubbing at them. He peered into the shop. He supposed a mouse was out of the question for a birthday present. Fiona would kill him.

He shut his mind, once again, on the many things Fiona might be tempted to say to him today.

Anyway, Ella and Larry already had a guinea pig and a rabbit. The first time he went to their house Stephen sat on the back deck, looking down at the view, feeling the great luxury of Fiona's ex-husband's wealth lapping over him with the breeze and the sound of the water. Then Larry, the younger daughter, had appeared beside his chair, clutching something long and furred at her chest.

'Oh!' he'd said, making a child-greeting smile. 'Hello!'

His voice was awkward; he had not been ready for this. And then he saw that the column of fur was a live rabbit. Larry held the creature under its forelegs, elbows at her sides, her fingers meeting as she clasped it, as if it were a posy of flowers.

Stephen yelped. Larry and the rabbit both stared at him in silence. He watched the rabbit's glazed gaze from its brown eyes, its long body dangling down the little girl's front. It didn't struggle or shiver, merely hung there, resigned, its soft, pouchy skin bunching up around its neck. Was Stephen supposed to do something? He leaned back, away from its fur. Larry just stared, her jaw set, blinking now and then in the sun. He heard himself babble. 'What a lovely rabbit! Is it yours?'

She said nothing, but moved her jaw to one side, then nodded. She shifted a little, hitching the rabbit up as though it were a piece of clothing.

'What's its name?' Stephen was worried now, not about his allergy but about the rabbit. Perhaps it was going into some sort of catatonic trauma, its blood supply halted. It hung, like a pelt.

Larry stared at him with her slightly bulging, wide blue eyes, and looked as if she might cry. She said, in a low, gravelly voice: 'Fluffy.'

'Hello, Fluffy!' Stephen said, hearing his woodenness. 'Do you think he might like to go back to his cage now?' He looked around for Fiona, but she was nowhere to be seen.

Larry shook her head. 'Oh,' said Stephen. 'It's a girl,' croaked Larry.

'Ah,' Stephen said. He swallowed. The rabbit swallowed too. Then Larry whirled and ran off down the side of the house, the rabbit's body stretching and bouncing softly as she ran, the breeze billowing her little purple dress.

Stephen had slumped in his chair, a simmer of unease beginning in him. What was he doing there anyway? Fiona was his ex-brother-in-law's sister; could there be a more tangled and foolish thing to consider, than what he was considering?

There had been something erotic about it from the start, all those years ago when they danced together at Mandy and Chris's wedding, and snuck out to share a line of speed Fiona had brought. At the end of the evening they took another bottle of wine from the ice crate and drank it on the back steps of Stephen's parents' house, talking and laughing and smoking furiously till dawn. Nothing had happened between them, but whenever the memory returned his gut had fizzed with recalled anticipation. After the wedding, on the three or four times they met over the years there had been a fond, enthusiastic embrace, a lively clinking of glasses.

But well over a decade then passed without them seeing each other, and in that time Mandy and Chris divorced, Chris had remarried. Fiona had long finished uni, become a physiotherapist at one of the big teaching hospitals, married and then unmarried a barrister. And had two kids.

They had met again by accident at the zoo kiosk counter, the little girls behind her at one of the iron tables, stuffing chips into themselves. The promising warmth in Fiona's eyes across the counter, the instant flirtatious revival of the possibility that had always been there, made him catch his breath. He'd watched her stride back to her bag on the table for a pen, observed her as she bent over the counter to write down his phone number. He found he wanted to bury his fingers in the thick sandy scruff of her short, surfie-boy's hair. He wanted to touch the fine sheen of sweat on her brow. As she bent to write and the neckline of her blue cotton sundress fell open, he saw the soft cleft between her breasts, and he wanted to fit his thumb to that space, just there.

When she moved back to the table and her chattering girls, gathering up the strewn detritus of their lunch, his boss Russell saw him watching.

'Who's she?' Russell said too loudly.

'Just someone I used to know,' Stephen murmured, turning away to wipe the counter.

'Bit mumsy, isn't she?' said Russell, considering her as she began to push Larry's stroller up the sloping path, calling to Ella over her shoulder.

Russell, like most men, would never notice what Stephen found so arousing in Fiona. She was too circumspect, too guardedly dressed, for one thing—Russell liked unambiguous short skirts and bouncy cleavages. But in seeing her again Stephen was undone, just as in their youth, by her direct, mischievous gaze; the sceptical way she listened to him talk, biting her lip a little to keep from smiling. She had a held-back quality, a hiddenness, that to Stephen—along with her slender, strong brown arms, the quick, graceful movement of her smooth calves as she walked—was sexy as hell. An old, old lust sprang up in him.

On his way out of the zoo that day Stephen paused to watch one of the keepers feeding a hummingbird from his cupped hand. The little bird whirred and hovered, darting in and out to the keeper's motionless upturned palm. A drab little bird with a black throat, until it moved again and the light struck differently, and for the briefest instant its throat flashed iridescent red, then dulled again. The watchers gasped, waiting for that miniature glory to reveal itself once more, but the colour vanished, the bird cocked its head and moved away. Fiona was like this, Stephen thought then. The ruby-throated hummingbird. If you waited, if you carefully watched, she might show you a glimpse of this gorgeousness, this vividness. And you wanted nothing more than to see it again.

But two *kids*, he'd thought, sitting on her deck that afternoon. Let alone the awkwardness of their own siblings' marital history. Suddenly there by his side Larry reappeared. This time she gripped a scrabbling guinea pig to her chest. 'Oh,' Stephen said weakly. Where the hell was Fiona?

The guinea pig wriggled and struggled in Larry's little hands, which formed a vice-like band around its body. She gave Stephen the same slightly hostile stare. 'And what's this one's name?' Stephen said, praying for the guinea pig to calm down, or else escape.

'Smooth.'

'And it's a—'

'Boy!' She looked scornfully at Stephen. He nodded; he could feel sweat in his armpits. The guinea pig had stopped struggling now. Perhaps she had killed it. But then it suddenly began again, and Larry bent her head, whispering '*Nuh*-uh,' into her chest. Her tone was not cruel, rather that of a firm, patient nurse, but still she squashed the animal's little body against herself, to calm or disable it.

The glass door to the house slid open; relief flooded through Stephen at the sound. But when he turned towards it, it was not Fiona striding towards him but Ella, the older girl, who had earlier stood behind her mother when she greeted him at the front door. Ella had changed her clothes from the t-shirt and shorts and now wore a pink floral dress with a bow around the middle. Her blonde hair floated around her head in a knotted staticky halo, as if she had begun to brush it but then lost heart. She did not look at him or speak as she flew past him, seemingly on her way to something important, but paused briefly to fling a plastic heart-shaped bowl on the table. It was filled with compost, fruit and vegetable scraps; some sludgy lumps of watermelon, a bent and bruised parsley stem, shreds of apple skin and banana and other unidentifiable flesh.

'Ah,' Stephen called brightly to Ella's disappearing back, 'old Smooth will love that.' But she was gone, and only Larry stood at the edge of the deck, the guinea pig put away now, her hands by her sides. Then Ella reappeared, joining her sister. They stood together, staring at Stephen in curious revulsion.

And finally, thank Christ, Fiona emerged from the house with a jug of water and glasses.

Ella, emboldened, cried out in contempt: 'It's not for *Smooth*,' and fled. Larry cast one last dark glance his way before following her sister, flouncing away down the side of the house.

Fiona was amused, sitting down beside him and laying her cool hand on the back of his neck. They both looked at the bowl of sludge. 'It's fruit salad,' she said. 'She made it for you.'

He stood in the delicious cool of the darkened food court and breathed, eyes still stinging. Most of the shops had not yet opened; there was an unaccustomed peace in the gloom. The girls would be all right, he had already decided. Children were resilient. Adults did not like to accept this, but Stephen knew it to be true, as he made his way to the centre's toilets. Children understood more intelligently than adults that all things passed. They would bounce back. They would forget him in a couple of weeks.

Would Fiona ever let him see them again?

He stood in the dank toilet air, lathering his hands and forearms with soap, rinsing away Balzac's sticky hair-dust, the heat and the sweat. It was only eight o'clock and he was half a block from his own house, but already the dog, the city, had layered him with grime and pathogens and sweat. He bent low over the basin and stared at the porcelain, left the tap running and splashed cold water again and again onto his face. He blinked and squinted the water into his wide open eyes, sluicing it all around his eyeballs, filling the lids and sockets. Then he screwed them tightly shut, splashed his face again and again, and stood grimacing, the water running down to soak the neck of his t-shirt. He ran his cool, wet hands back and forth over his head and face and neck. He breathed out, stood up straight and looked into the mirror. His eyes were rimmed red, as if he'd been crying. But he felt better. He rubbed at his nose one last time, and pushed out of the toilet door into the great cavern of the shopping centre.

In Kmart he stared at the shelves of My Little Ponies. Ella and Larry were infatuated with this junk. They had My Little Pony toys—hard plastic ones, soft fluffy ones—and books and DVDs and lunch boxes and drink bottles, but still they begged and whined for more every time one of the nauseating My Little Pony ads came on the television. But which to get?

Standing here in the industrial draught of the Kmart air-conditioning he learned there were many different ponies, called Starsong and Sweetie Belle and Rainbow Dash and Pinkie Pie. They had wide, hoofless feet, tiny little bodies and wide flat heads with enormous, freakishly lashed eyes. But the essential part of the My Little Pony was the hair. Every pony's luxuriant, roiling, pink and purple nylon mane was longer than the pony's height, and each had a pink and purple nylon tail, equally long, to match. Each Pony came with a set of hair accessories: hairbrushes, combs, ribbons, hairclips, extensions and tiaras. The lushly curled hairstyles of the ponies reminded Stephen of the slightly dangerous bombshells who lolled over velvet chaise longues in the midday movies of his childhood—Zsa Zsa Gabor, Mrs Robinson. Stephen had tried to follow the logic of the ponies' peculiarly female world. They stood on their hind legs and carried handbags. They lived in Ponyville, in mansions made of 'candy'. There were also smaller, baby Little Ponies that wore *diapers* and sucked on *pacifiers*. They all visited fun parks, rode Ferris wheels. When Ella explained that whenever the ponies visited the sea they magically became beautiful mermaids, Stephen gave up.

He reached up and grasped hold of a My Little Pony Cheeri-Lee Ponyville Supermarket Store Playset.

At the Mexican sandwich shop the tanned, muscle-bound young Vietnamese man—his tag said his name was Irving—twitched his hips as he frothed milk for coffee, head to toe in snug black fabric like a dancer, shimmying along to the music grinding out. '*Woohooo!*' he shouted now, wiggling his bum in time to a Michael Jackson drumbeat.

Two Chinese women who ran the cut-price linen outlet nearby were putting out displays of towels and pillows; the optometrist opening his glass door chatted with his neighbour at the Mr Minit stand. A Muslim woman in a pastel blue headscarf and leopard-print gown pushed a supermarket trolley with a garden rake sticking out of it. Across the food court, beyond Sushi Magic and the Gourmet Pizza Haven (*Friday special: Madras curry pizza*), Stephen saw the Plaza security guard watching her. The guard made his rounds of the shopping centre on one of those strange, two-wheeled vehicles with the low platform and a long vertical pole with handlebars. It made him look as if he were standing at a lectern, ready to deliver a speech. Stephen could walk the length of the whole centre in five minutes, but the security guard zoomed between duties—whatever they were—standing on his ridiculous vehicle with its giant wheels, spine rod-straight, staring unflinchingly ahead. The guard began to follow the Muslim lady at a distance on his little machine. Did the guard have duties in case of a terrorist attack, Stephen wondered? The only memorable attack—last year's ram raid—took place in the middle of the night. The next morning a giant red Pajero sat in the middle of the food court, broken glass everywhere. Stephen delighted in the brashness of it, the automatic teller machines on their sides, tyre marks on the lino. The guard had patrolled the perimeter of the police-taped food court on his Segway all day long. Now he followed the Muslim lady and her rake until she reached the exit, then swivelled on his machine, looking about for another disturbance.

Sticky-taped to the drinks cabinet behind Irving was a photocopied flyer advertising a circus. *African lions Monkeys Llamas, camels, geese liberty horses and performing bears*. There were also trapeze artists, acrobats and clowns. *Tickets here*.

Stephen's family had once driven all the way to Sydney to see the famous Moscow Circus. He and Cathy and Mandy boasted to their school friends for what felt like months in advance; to Stephen it seemed the whole town of Rundle thrilled at the idea. The Connolly children would be taken out of school for two days, be driven the nine hours to the city to see this miraculous show, would stay *in a hotel*, and be driven home again the next day.

He remembered only a few fragments of the actual circus: some swollen bears lumbering about, the sweet smell of fried food, the unfamiliar warmth of the air. He recalled spotlights and a feeling of risk, fearing the matted-overcoat bears even though they were far below in the dusty ring, waddling about on their hind legs in silly ruffs and hats, skipping rope and dancing waltzes with clowns in dinner suits.

But he remembered the occasion of it, the specialness of being taken. His parents' awe at their own profligacy; the inordinate, reckless pleasure they could not afford.

Forget the stupid Little Pony. He would take Ella to the circus. It would be her birthday gift; his last gift. He would take them both, sit with them on a hard wooden bench in a circus tent in the middle of a suburban sports oval, their soft weights pressing on either side of him, the smell of popcorn in the air, the dusty floodlit spectacle of lions, llamas, camels and geese before them. The girls would remember it—remember *him*—when they were grown. Fiona would have to let them come. Surely.

Irving pressed down the plastic lid on Stephen's coffee, and called over the music, 'Still workin' same place, mate?' as he held out his hand for money, still boogying. The circus tickets now lay on the counter.

'Huh?' said Stephen. They had never discussed Stephen's job, but Irving jerked his head towards the cafe across the food court, his collegiate tone indicating he mistook Stephen for a fellow Plaza worker.

'La Villagio, isn't it?' said Irving.

Stephen was confused. 'No,' he said, sliding the tickets into his wallet and reaching for the coffee. He didn't like friendly chat with shopkeepers. 'I work at the zoo.'

'Oh, sorry,' Irving chirped. 'Thought you were a chef.'

Stephen realised Irving was looking at his trousers. This had happened before.

'Ah. They're not chef's pants. They're just pants, with checks,' he said. 'I got them at Aldi.'

Irving looked doubtful for a second, but he said, 'All right,' and beamed past Stephen at the next customer.

Near the exit a gaggle of old people sat in food court chairs waiting, vigilant, for the Aldi doors to open. Stephen liked the lucky-dip nature of the German supermarket's layout. One day you might find a basket of children's lifejackets, and the next day, in its place would be a high stack of office binding machines, or men's sequinned waistcoats. The pants had appealed to Stephen—clean black and white checks, with a wide band of elastic at the waist. They were eleven dollars; he bought two pairs. They were not chef's pants.

Stephen realised now that back in the street Jill had also given his pants a suspicious once-over. But they were just pants. He tugged his t-shirt further down below his waistline and sucked at the teat on the coffee lid.

His path was suddenly blocked by a young woman with ginger dreadlocks, wearing green army pants and boots and holding a clipboard. 'Do you care about animals, sir?' she asked sweetly. He half-nodded at the floor, trying to scoot past her. But unlike the Save the Children people who'd call 'Thank you have a nice day' to your back when you ignored them, this woman was not to be deterred. She sidestepped; he had to stop walking or plough into her.

'We're trying to stop the exploitation and degradation of animals in our society.' Friendly, challenging. 'And we need your help.'

'Ah, right,' he said. 'Trouble is, I'm late for work.' A man scurried by, visibly gleeful at his own escape.

'Oh, I *totally* know, and I won't hold you up for more than a second.' She gave him a wide, sensuous smile. Her name was Savannah. She shook his hand as if they were meeting at a party. Stephen sighed, and told her his name.

'Do you care about animals, Stephen?' Savannah asked again in an interested way, as if she were asking did he eat almonds, or what was his favourite movie; as if it were possible for Stephen to answer no, he did not, and be on his way.

She smiled up at him in calm contemplation. Her dull reddish hair poked in matted strands from her head. An ugly brown rock hung from a fine silver circle around her neck, and below the rock Stephen noticed the pleasant, natural press of her breasts against her black singlet top. He quickly looked back to her face. Her nose was pierced with a green stone, and she wore big silver loops in her ears. She was freckled and small, but strong. Something in her stance—her optimism, her apparent belief in him, held him there. Even as he began rummaging in his mind for an excuse for not giving her money, he found he was glad of Savannah and her youth, that the world had people like her in it.

Just then she began flipping the laminated pages of a terrible book in her hands. Stephen's goodwill evaporated. He did not want to see them, the foggy images of trapped and tortured beasts. He had never actually looked at such photographs, though he was always grimly aware of their presence on a sandwich board at a market or stuck to the wall in a health food shop. At those times it was easy to avert his eyes, grateful that the quality of the photographs was always so poor (he supposed they were taken on mobile phones by reckless vigilante saboteurs at night) that even if you came across one without expecting it, it was easy to avoid the detail. His general impression now of the photographs at the periphery of his vision, as Savannah turned her stiff pages, was the same: murky, pink and black, gloomy shapes, blurred close-ups of mouths and ears and patches of red, all contrasting with the steely grey lines of instruments or bars.

And now Savannah's throaty voice took on the urgent, moral tone he knew would come. His scalp prickled. He was being manipulated, yet at the same time he knew that what was done to these animals was the fault of him and others like him: cruel meat-eaters, gluttons too greedy for their own pleasure to spare a second's pity for the enslaved providers of their food, their medicines. No matter the cause—Save the Children, the Wilderness Society, Amnesty International—Stephen accepted that blame for the world's ills could justifiably be laid at his feet. The question here, now, with Savannah, was how to show compassion, how to show her he was different from everybody else, and still hang on to his cash.

He stared absently at the curve where Savannah's smooth neck met her shoulder as she went on talking. He began to dislike her now. Wealthy family, he decided. Stockbrokers or lawyers for parents. The only rebel lesbian in her year at one of the posh girls' schools, but still living with her parents in the lush suburbs, one of those mansions with electric gates and a Merc in the garage, which she would scorn and lecture her parents about except when she needed a lift to a festival of films about Uighurs or arms dealers in Afghanistan.

Behind her the butchers shunted trays of pink meat into display cabinets, leaning inside the glass to yank the long fringes of green plastic grass into place between the trays. There were tubs of sticky-looking indistinguishable marinated meats in soy dark or lurid orange, and rafts of pale, mealy-looking sausages. Stephen could smell it: the dank, rude odour of raw flesh. Sometimes he wondered, about meat: what if this were human flesh? Would his own thigh meat look and taste like this?

Last week, as Fiona's knife worked doggedly through a thick layer of pork rind and fat, he heard her give a small gasp. They both stared for a moment at the hard little nipple looking back at them from the chopping board: tender, clean and pink as Fiona's own. She stared down at it, stricken. 'I can't cut it off,' she whispered. Stephen said quickly, 'Let's not look,' and flipped the piece of belly over. After a moment Fiona went on working at the meat, but the strange discomfort remained in the air, and at dinner they exchanged a look before cutting into the soft, sweet meat.

Fiona had told him something else once: that after Larry was born by Caesarean, the doctors had worked away beyond the sheet at her waist to close her up. She lay there with the baby on her breast, tearful and exhausted, while they cauterised something, some part inside her. Fiona's grey eyes widened and her voice dropped to a whisper as she told him: 'It smelled like a *barbecue*.'

She thought it grotesque, and Stephen felt faint with horror at the idea of her soft, creamy belly carved into with knives—how they had touched her, pushed into that same soft part of her that he cradled with his hand as he curled behind her in bed. The idea of such invasion was dreadful.

It was when he touched the curved, glassy scar—afterwards, that first time in bed—that he saw she had learned to protect herself. She lifted his hand away from the scar, slowly drew up her knees to curl on her side and face him, his hand held between both of hers. She gazed at him, and he understood that life had toughened her. Childbirth had done it, and marriage, divorce.

Her husband had wanted a girl, not a grown-up, she told Stephen. And so he found one, at work. The first time she'd got past it, for the sake of the girls, but after that it was impossible.

'I can't do that little-girl, wifey shit anymore. I'm an adult now,' she said calmly. And in the jut of her chin, the gentle seriousness in her eyes, Stephen saw how hard won was her strength, and what courage it had taken for her to come to him, how fiercely she wanted his desire. For the first time in his life he found himself wanting to live up to something—to meet her, to take this beautiful risk—and it made the wave of his need for her crest and break again, unashamed and glorious. And as she rose above him in the dark he glimpsed it again, the ruby-throated bird. He lay awake beside her all night, falling in love.

But bodies, he thought now, watching the butchers hefting flesh, didn't matter. Fiona's story about the cooking smell had not unnerved him in that way: he was unfazed by the knowledge that human beings were made of meat. In fact—he had never voiced this, but—more and more he thought that surely any immorality in eating animals would vanish if it were permissible to eat people too.

Perhaps he should share his theory now, with Savannah. She lifted her avid, righteous gaze to him. He decided not.

'Ask yourself a simple question, Stephen. Does your palate or pleasure or fashion sense justify the suffering or death of another creature?'

She waited. He was forced now to look down at the picture she held open. In some gloomy darkness, a huge sow lay on its side on a concrete floor behind thick stainless steel bars. The pig's belly faced the camera, pressed up against the bars so its legs and teats stuck through the rails. In the foreground of the picture four little piglets, separated from their mother by the bars, suckled at the sow's teats through the gaps. The animal's eyes were open; it stared into the middle distance. Lying helpless on the cold floor, its expression was unmistakable: the pig was in sheer and utter misery.

'That's . . . terrible,' Stephen murmured, looking away.

The poor creature, his mother would say (why could he not shake off the burden of her, this of all mornings?). She said it often, about everyone; a neighbour with the flu or a murdered policeman on the television news, it didn't matter. *Poor creature* was for all suffering, everywhere.

Savannah's eyes shone. '*Yes,*' she said, triumphant. 'It is.'

She sighed then, as if this simple admission was all she wanted from Stephen, all she wanted from anybody. They stood there together. Her sudden stillness made Stephen wonder what other people said when she made them look at the picture. That the image was doctored, perhaps, or this one was an aberration, or that the animal didn't mind.

There was no way out now. He slid the credit card from his wallet and signed over fifteen bucks a month for the promotion of animal rights.

Savannah bent to fill out the paperwork, glowing, it seemed, with the shock of her success. Stephen thought grandly that there might even be something a bit like love for him in her gratitude. He stole a glance down the curve of her spine to where her army trousers gaped to show the soft, inviting hollow of her bum. But he looked away quickly before she stood up. He was aware now that women knew when you looked at their bums or their boobs. Fiona had set him straight on that one time, laughing at his denials and blushes.

Savannah ripped the form off her pad of tiny-print credit-card forms and thrust them at him. As he folded the page into a small grey wad, regretting the fifteen bucks already, Savannah asked him: 'Off to a shift then? Where do you work?'

'The zoo,' he said.

She blinked, looked him up and down.

'These aren't chef's pants,' he said. 'I'm not a chef.'

He extended his hand but she drew back from him, shaking her dreadlocks slowly in disbelief. Then, before he even said goodbye, she leapt in front of a woman with a pram. 'Does your little girl like animals, madam?'

As the doors slid open a great draught of scorched air greeted him—how suffocating, how impossibly *airless* it was—along with the wheelchair man's hoots of repugnant, vulgar laughter.

Stephen was blooming with resentment about Savannah's horrified glare, the money he had given her. He could not save the *Big Issue* woman today; there was only so much he could do. Already the weight of his guilt pressed down upon him like layers of earth. His mother loomed, with her humming secret. Fiona's face flashed once, staring at him in the same disbelief as Savannah's, before he brought a shutter down upon the image. The only way he could reach the end of this day was not to allow such visions. He could not.

Charlotte Wood

If only Stephen were braver, a better man, he would say something to the wheelchair man. But he passed them with his head down, his bag heavy and his jaw set with shame. And then he saw something strange. The *Big Issue* woman was laughing, and she put out a hand to touch the wheelchair man's arm.

Stephen didn't understand it. She wasn't trapped. She and the wheelchair man were having a whale of a time.

CHAPTER 2

Cambridge Road was always a bottleneck in the mornings. He was a little late now. Usually he did not mind the slow start to the morning's drive across the city. You could allow the traffic to carry you in a sort of reverie, crawling in a lulling forward roll, half a car length at a time, motor idling and your mind free to wander. But today he did not welcome the meanderings of his mind. He must stay composed. He peered out at the shops, watching the Norton morning coming alive.

The Cat Protection Society op shop door hung open. Stephen supposed the shop was run by crazy old women, the kind who hoarded cats. Men were cruel to animals with kicks and blows, but it was women who starved them to death. Gathering them by the hundred, allowing their houses to fill with shit and piss, watching the creatures weaken, sicken, day by day.

This was why he had to do what he must today. A single sharp blow was surely preferable to the misery of slow starvation. Fiona would see. He was being kind.

The open door offered a glimpse inside the shop: a gloomy corridor between a rack of heavy wool coats and shelves of ugly handmade pottery. Stephen didn't have to see further to know what else would be in there: shelves of books on microwave cookery, flesh-coloured Stable Tables, with their saggy, discoloured beanbag undersides, for bedridden invalids to rest their dinner plates on. The stippled tubs of 'foot spas' manufactured in grubby pale-blue plastic, as if the colour might somehow evoke the sea instead of the fungal dust of elderly strangers' pumiced heels.

Stephen saw the homeless man who sometimes crouched in a little nest of dirty blankets across the road from Stephen's house. Tangle-haired, grizzled, he squatted now against the Cat Protection Society's tiled wall, a filthy bag beside him.

Stephen's car rolled forward.

A woman sat smoking on a plastic chair outside the hairdresser, in a lurid pink nylon cape and a cement-coloured helmet. Strands of plastered hair stood out from her head like electrodes as she squinted and sucked at her fag. She was one of Norton's people, the people in tracksuits and logo-covered working clothes: the men with hard, chiselled calf muscles and lurid orange or green occupational health and safety vests, the women in tight black skirts and pastel singlets and thick-heeled, rubber-soled sandals that were somehow sluttish and practical at once. There were two populations in Norton—this world, of fiercely sucking smokers outside shops and pizza-eaters over garbage bins, and then the others—the inner city vintage freelance crowd. These were gaunt men with scruffy hair and fastidiously shabby fashion sense, the kind who carried fat happy babies on their shoulders when they shopped, whose black and grey clothes looked old even when new, who worked from studios at home as architects or freelance lighting designers. The women of this crowd seemed to have given up caring how they looked, except for the fact they all looked the same. Stephen studied them in supermarket queues and listened to their conversations. They did Pilates and had blunt fringes, wore small rectangular glasses and Japanese-looking clothes so severely ugly you knew they were expensive. These were editors or radio producers or consultants who wrote policy on restorative justice. You heard them greeting each other in the mall; they rolled their eyes to cover the embarrassment of being discovered in the food court (they blamed their children); they always kissed each other hello. They called their work *my project*. They were the kind of people who didn't like to be thought wealthy even if they were—this was an inner-city phenomenon, unlike the beachside suburbs or Longley Point where Fiona lived, where being thought wealthy was the aim of the game.

The two populations of Norton were ghosts to one another as they brushed past each other in the streets, at the automatic teller or the supermarket queue, the air between them barely riffling.

He drew alongside Foam City, where he'd bought Fiona's yoga mat.

Fiona *loved* yoga, she would sigh, almost every time she floated in the door after her Wednesday evening class. And she did seem different after these classes—the whirring energy in her was temporarily stilled, she moved more slowly, was less provoked by the bickering of the girls. Except last Wednesday, that was. When she had walked in and hurled her bag down on the couch, swearing. 'Can you *believe*,' she raged pouring a huge glass of wine, 'that this woman *laughed* at me!'

The new teacher, it seemed, had urged Fiona to try a headstand.

'But I was scared of falling,' she said. 'So I just made this tiny hopeless little hop, instead of getting my legs right up, and then this woman next to me, flexible as hell, you know—spent half the class with her chin on the floor—she bursts out into this little *snigger* at me!' Fiona gulped the wine. 'But then I looked at her and I thought, well, you might be able to do a headstand but you've got a fat arse.'

Stephen laughed out loud, but Fiona was actually, truly offended. She took a big swig from the glass again and swallowed, wiped her mouth with her hand, and then peered into the pot of gluggy pasta sauce Stephen had made for the girls.

When she turned back she sighed, twisting the glass stem in her hands. 'That wasn't very yogic of me, was it,' she said glumly. 'But she was a bitch.'

From the couch both girls turned eagerly at this, calling, 'You said the B-word!' They adored catching adults swearing.

Stephen had sworn a lot when Fiona had tried to teach him yoga a few times, the two of them cross-legged on the living room floor, following the instructions of an American yoga teacher called Dawnelle on a DVD. He liked the lessons, but only so he could watch Fiona. He liked the careful way she laid out her little yoga things around her—a purple cushion, a wheat-filled eye bag, an ugly grey blanket—and then lay down with her eyes shut, an obedient rod, before the DVD began. She refused to fast-forward any of it, even the boring music at the start. Stephen found the poses impossible; his body wouldn't accommodate even the most basic ones—even simply sitting cross-legged, his knees pointed at the ceiling while Fiona's limbs were fluid, her knees horizontal—and his inability made him feel stupid.

But Fiona's concentration was absolute. Her effort, as she turned her body into the inverted V, her face growing red as she struggled to hold the pose for yet another minute, moved him. Her tracksuit pants would slip down her hips and her t-shirt would ruck up. The tremor in her legs and elbows, her belly rising and falling, her eyes closed, lips softly closing and opening for breathing exactly as Dawnelle instructed; all this sent a shard of love through Stephen every time.

Fiona carried a tiny, flimsy little mint-green mat to classes, but to Stephen's eye it was useless; hardly a thing at all, thin as a sheet. So he went to Foam City to get her the best yoga mat he could find, choosing a two-inch thick sheet of black industrial rubber. *Bigger*, he said when the salesman indicated where he would cut. He wrestled the coiled thing into the back of his ute, and then through the front door of Fiona's house one afternoon, getting it almost to the living room before it unfurled with a mighty *whump*, filling the width and half the length of the hallway.

'It's *huge*,' Fiona crowed, clutching his arm. 'It's hilarious!' She lay down on it in the hallway, and the girls came running to bounce up and down along its length before collapsing, throwing themselves over her. She groaned and shrieked, and they all lay there, beaming up at him. His girls. Later Stephen heard Fiona telling someone he had given her the best yoga mat *ever*. 'It's like doing yoga in a jumping castle!' she cried into the phone. He felt a glow of pride inside himself for days.

His car rolled on, stopped, rolled. The traffic wave carried him forward, stopped again.

So what had happened? That's what she would ask him. How had things changed so much, what was the difference between then—only two months ago—and now? He felt his jaw clench, the nausea lapping. He couldn't say. It just was.

He sighed. Please, oh please let this day be ended.

The doctor. That's what the skimming fear was, to do with his mother. *The doctor said . . . especially now.* Stephen gripped the wheel. She never mentioned doctors to Stephen, though Cathy was always on about some ailment that supposedly plagued their mother, the various pills she took. But Cathy worked in a pharmacy, she was obsessed with drugs. Still, it pressed at him. Margaret knew Stephen hated any mention of doctors, or hospitals. Especially since their father—but he would not be dragged back to that, that room, that bed, not today. He trawled back through his mother's words. 'Especially now.' Was she trying to hint at something too awful for direct speech? Is that why she had gotten so wound up about the bloody party? He tried to think. She said she had *sent him a link* about it. Was it possible there had been some news Stephen had simply missed? Surely Cathy would have berated him about it. But it was possible. For did he not spend his life trying to make sure of it, trying to escape from the knowledge of awful things?

Stephen rested his face in his hands for a moment. He breathed, then lifted his head, returned his hands to the wheel. Of course it was stupid. His mother was perfectly fine. She was old. One day she would die, but not yet. He made himself stare back into the Foam City window. COUCH CUSHIONS! CUT TO ORDER! Why did it feel that he had never, till this moment, considered the fact that his mother would die? Malevolent jellyfish blobs of bitter green polystyrene hung in the Foam City window. His skin chilled under the air-conditioning's blast.

Fiona would be home from the beach now. Thinking of her swimming calmed him. Sometimes she looked down at her body with despair, like the time after the smiling Thai waiter at their regular Tuesday night restaurant had noticed the little pot of her belly and asked her, delighted, if she was pregnant. She blushed a fierce red as she laughed it off, saying gaily, 'No, just fat,' waving away the waiter's embarrassed, bowing apologies. Stephen saw her swallowing tears, and her smile was tight until they left the restaurant. But in water, Fiona's body came sensuously alive; she swam in a strong, easy stroke, lounging in the water, utterly at ease. Each morning the girls went next door for half an hour while Fiona took the five-minute drive to the beach in her bathers, strode down to the sand and kicked off her thongs. She dropped the car key on its pink tag on to the towel, pulled a yellow rubber swimming cap down over her ears as she marched to the water. She high-stepped purposefully through the shallows, and as soon as the water reached her knees she launched herself and dived.

The first time Stephen watched her do this, he was seized with marvelling lust. That first time, when Fiona had called to him and he swam out to her, the light, shameful fear rose in him as it always did when his feet could not touch the bottom. He had grasped her slippery body and she held him too, mistaking his grip on her for one of desire, and she laughed when he joked about his fear of water, about his having been an inland child—the ghastly lessons at the Rundle pool, and the swimming carnival near-drownings. She thought he was exaggerating; he could never speak to her of the real fear that gripped him when a wave rose before him, when all he could see before it gripped and hurled him was the yellow beacon of her cap, and he fought the panic in himself while he gasped and pedalled water, floundering back to shore. Where he would thrust the air back out of his lungs and force his heartbeat slow again, and pretend he had not been terrified.

Now they took the girls to the beach together, and Fiona would swim out to the perilous dark water, slipping over and under the waves in her sleek dips and dives while Stephen splashed in the foaming shallows with the kids, crouching and shouting with them as the waves broke about his hips. Lifting the girls high—first one, then the other, both Larry and Ella kicking and shrieking with thrill, shouting *throw me, throw me!* He would throw them, chilled with fear himself every time as he watched them fall and plunge, and he would be on the verge of diving to find them when they would burst up, water streaming from their wide grinning mouths and the starfish lashes of their open blue eyes.

It was after one of these swims when they sat on the sand, the girls squatting on their heels digging holes nearby, that Fiona had suggested Stephen move into her place.

He squinted at the water while his breath caught, and then made a joke about being terrible at housework. He felt her waiting for him to meet her gaze, while he watched the girls. He stared and stared at them, but could not look at her. Then she said, quite calmly, 'It's okay, Stephen. You don't have to.' And she'd got up and walked back to the water and flew beneath a wave, and was gone. Then Larry had leapt up and run, and Ella followed her across the white crush of the ocean's edge. They were like their mother: they hurled themselves to the waves, while Stephen sat on the sand, helpless with apprehension and envy. Fiona had not mentioned it again.

The cars crawled towards the traffic lights at Hunter Street. Last week at these lights he had seen a man leap from his car and charge up to the driver's window of the vehicle in front of him, screaming *you fucking moron,* and then, lightning-fast, throw a punch through the open window. The car had suddenly screeched off against the lights, on the wrong side of the road—Stephen admired the driver's quick thinking—and left the punching man standing alone in the street. He had had to walk back across the empty space to his car with its door hanging open, watched by all the waiting traffic, and get in, close the door, and edge the vehicle forward and wait with the rest of them.

The lights changed, finally, and Stephen accelerated across the intersection; moving, at last, into the day. But then a noise, his foot plunged to the brake. Something had happened, was happening. Something flapped above his car; a huge, ungainly bird filled the windscreen. It sailed above his bonnet, and he saw then that the thing was a woman. Her eyes lightly closed, head tilted skywards, mouth agape. Cars spun past in the four lanes of Cambridge Road, swerving around his, sounding horns. Stephen understood he had hit her. The body—the jeans, zippered grey tracksuit top, the tiny head with its dull brown fur—plummeted to the bitumen before his car. The clothes and body bounced—how *bounce?*—and there was the face again, eyes wide, mouth yawning in laughter or a scream. Stephen sat in his seat, foot jammed hard on the brake, hands gripping the steering wheel, the car skew-whiff on the axis of its lane, trying to fathom what the fuck had happened to him now.

A dreadful wail rose up; the woman was somehow scuttling to the side of the road, crouched low, dragging herself through gaps in the lurching traffic. Stephen skipped through the cars, found himself kneeling beside her on the side of the road, his car abandoned behind him, door open, in the centre lane. Cars slowed but kept moving, horns sounding, accelerating away.

He shouted: 'Are you alright?'

She could not possibly be alright. She lay, her little shorn head in the gutter, her long thin body sideways, skinny black-jeaned legs weirdly angled. She moaned, her long body churning in the gutter. He looked for blood, registered relief at the sound of her crying.

Stephen stared at her stretched open mouth, one bony hand clutching at her shoulder. 'Me *aarm*, me*yarm*,' she wailed, and Stephen heard his own panicked shouting, 'Just wait,' as if she could go anywhere, and he scampered across the lanes back through the horns and the cars, shut the door, put his feet on the pedals.

What he had just seen—the body falling like a doomed, plummeting kite—was a watermark over everything he saw now, and panic and blood rose in him. He forced it away with his own voice, aloud in the car: *keep calm don't fucking panic.* He edged the car to the kerb, all the time hearing another voice: *just go! just go!*

She was still in the gutter, her head now lolling horribly onto the footpath. Her eyes squinted shut, her mouth a wide grimace of pain. She had stopped wailing, and instead, much worse, grizzled like an animal, a long, dirt-coloured creature in black jeans and a thin grey singlet and the zippered tracksuit top, one grasshopper leg tucked beneath and the other bent above her. She panted, her cheek pushed into the kerb, her face the same colour as the concrete. Her right hand still clutched her left shoulder. She whimpered, 'Mefuckingarm, Jesus Christ!' Stephen could only repeat it, *Jesus Christ,* as he squatted, and then shouted, 'I'm going to lift you.'

He scooped her up and she yairled a high, animal shriek of pain—somehow his brain recalled a possum fight outside his window one midnight—and kept shrieking as he lowered her into the passenger seat, yanking his backpack into place to fashion a support for her head. He pushed her legs in and slammed the door. The voice in his head still shouted *Go. Go. Leave her.* And he understood finally that this voice came not from him but a taxi-driver across the road, pulled up by the kerb. Stephen stared in dumb confusion as he started the ignition; he saw the taxi-driver's face, red with frustration. The man shouted: 'It's just a fucking junkie! Her own fault! Just go!'

Stephen stared, uncomprehending. The taxi-driver shook his head, exasperated, and then swerved out from the gutter. Gone.

Stephen pulled out into the traffic again. 'We'll be at the hospital in one minute,' he called over the girl's whimpering, praying this to be true, thinking of the broken bones, the blood that must be swamping through her.

The girl slurred: 'No.' She was mad with pain, or worse. She closed her eyes again and sucked in breath through clenched teeth. Stephen accelerated, changed lanes. 'You have to go to hospital. You hit your head on the road.' *I hit your head on the road.* In a block he could turn left towards the hospital. Come on, come on, he whispered to the traffic. It crawled. *Fucking come on.* Her face was grey. Please don't die. He imagined the blood inside her skull, trickling and seeping, curling through the frills and furrows of the brain. He slowed and lurched to a stop as the car in front refused to run the orange light. Jesus, *Jesus* Christ. He leant on the horn.

The girl hissed with the car's lurching. Her eyes opened, then shut tight against pain, and she said, with effort, 'Me doctor's just down here, jes' take me there.'

'You have to go to *hospital*,' Stephen said. He jammed the horn again, began rolling down his window to wave at the driver in the next lane.

But the girl convulsed in her seat. She cried out, 'Just fucken STOP HERE.'

Stunned into obedience, Stephen swung the Subaru into a no-stopping zone beside Blockbuster Video, the sudden stop making the girl roar even louder. She was burrowing at the door, trying to open the latch with her broken arm! Stephen leapt out into the bright air and tore once more around the car, looking about him for the doctor's surgery.

He wrenched her door open. For an instant, seeing the girl cornered here in his car, Savannah's animal torture photographs returned to him: the grizzled narrow head, the thin face pocked and pierced and blotched, the panting mouth, eyes closed in pain and fear. He reached in and she let out a low, agonised howl as he dragged her out and stood her upright, grasping her round the waist, trying to support her weight without touching her injured side. Her head was on his shoulder; again he pictured the blood rushing and flooding through her skull. Maybe she would die here, in his arms. He stared into the city and had no idea what to do.

But the girl lifted her broken head and fixed her blurred gaze on an anonymous brown shopfront across the road. She jolted, launching herself out into the traffic. Stephen bellowed and clutched at her, dragging her backwards as a large silver four-wheel-drive thundered past. 'For fucksake! Stop *doing* that!' he roared, and then he wanted to punch her, and there was a break in the traffic and he ran, dragging her without care across the road.

When they reached the other side he shrieked at her: 'What are you fucking trying to do!' but she ignored him, steering toward the tinted door. He rushed to shove it open before she could use her damaged arm. The door closed behind them with a sucking thud, and they stood, clutching one another, sealed in the muggy silence of a tinted glass chamber. In front was another brown tinted glass door and beyond that, an empty waiting room. The girl cried out 'Pam!' and there was a loud buzz and they burst into the waiting room.

There were chairs, magazines, but no people. Stephen was lost. He stared at the girl, and then heard a woman say, 'G'day, Skye.' He whirled to see a high counter like a bank teller's, and more glass panels. Behind the counter an older woman gave him a brief, businesslike nod. Relief surged through him; here was someone older, someone medical and parental and sane.

'She needs a doctor!'

In the silence of the room, his shouted panic sounded foolish. The girl had lifted her weight from his arm and was standing unsupported. She had stopped making any noise at all. The girl—called Skye—now stood impossibly straight, her broken arm hanging almost naturally, and she called to the woman, 'I'm fine, Pam, I just need me dose.' Her grizzling and panting gone, her voice deliberately low, the only sign of her earlier agony a tense frown, her mouth held open, tongue running across her lower lip over and over in a rhythmic distraction from her pain.

Stephen began to yelp and babble. 'But she got hit by a car. *My* car. I hit her! She needs a *doctor.*'

Pam looked on doubtfully. She said to Stephen, 'Was she hurt?'

He shouted, 'She landed on her *head*,' but at the same time Skye's voice descended, calm and steely, over his: 'I'm fine, Pam, I just need me dose, please.'

'It's okay,' Pam said to Stephen. 'You can go.'

'But she needs a *doctor.*' He sounded hysterical.

Skye spoke in a fierce, threatening murmur: 'I'm fine, Pam, please. Me dose, please.' She didn't look at Stephen. He was of no use to her.

He wheeled round to Pam, begging. 'Please, she's got a smashed *head.*'

But Pam was already pushing a small paper cup across the counter to Skye. She looked up at Stephen and said, more kindly now, 'It's okay. You can go.'

Defeated, he found himself scribbling his phone number on the back of a supermarket docket. 'I have to go to work. But if you need to get in touch with me,' he said, his voice small. He held it out to Skye, who ignored him, reaching for the cup. The buzzer sounded again. Pam looked at him expectantly. He understood the buzzer was for the door. He put the paper with his number on the counter in front of Skye, and turned to go back out the way he came. The two women chorused, 'Other way,' and Pam pointed toward a new glass door across the room. The buzzing swelled and filled the space. He took one last look at Skye, now small in the big room, tipping the cup back as she drank. She did not look at him. And in an instant he was through the door and it fell heavily shut behind him and he was bumped outside again, onto Queen Street and the gritty summer humidity of Norton. He turned to look behind him but the methadone clinic was sealed off, hidden by thick mirrored glass, and all he could see was himself: stricken, sweaty, middle aged, gaunt in the face with thinning hair. He saw the stretched red t-shirt, the sludge of flesh hanging over the waistband of the stupid chequered black-and-white pants. The dirty sneakers.

He stood, wondering what to do. Here on Norton's main street the only sounds were the weekday traffic, an ascending plane, and the clumsy three-chord strumming and off-key Elvis crooning of a homeless man busking outside the 7-Eleven.

Stephen's phone rang.

He looked at the thing in his hand. Here, from the distant universe of her Longley Point life, was Fiona. His whole body was swamped with relief. He wanted the capable nearness of her, his ally. He wanted to tell her everything: about the accident, his mother, about his dread of hurting her this afternoon. His feet burned in his sneakers.

'Hi,' he said tenderly into the phone. He clutched it in both hands, as if it might fly away, or fall.

But Fiona's voice was tense. 'It's me,' she said. 'Listen, what's wrong with your mother?'

He heard Larry in the background, yelling, *Pissoff! Pissoff!*

'Larry!' Fiona shouted away from the phone.

'What do you mean what's wrong with her?' Stephen asked, the tremor in his guts growing stronger. The white pavement was smudged with small grey discs of old grease and chewing gum. He wanted to lie down upon it, right now, and sleep.

'She just called me,' Fiona said irritably. 'She asked whether we were coming up next weekend and I said as far as I knew, yes. She sounded weird. Why is she calling me about it? She's your mother.'

Stephen for the first time fully understood the word 'dumbstruck'. It was intelligence, and words, that were struck away.

'I don't know,' was all he said.

Piss off bumhead, shouted Larry. It's a mistake, he wanted to say. I don't want to leave you. I don't know why I'm going to.

He said: 'What's Larry yelling at?'

'The little boy from next door. Aidan. Hang on. *Larry!*'

There was a pause while Fiona covered the phone and shouted at her daughter. Stephen tried to think of something to say.

'I didn't know you wanted to go,' he said, trying to make his voice normal. He was so tired, and so, so *hot*.

Fiona sighed, as if Stephen was another of her children. 'Look, all I know is it's on the calendar. Cathy asked us ages ago, remember? Your dad's birthday thing.'

'I didn't think you would want to go.'

'What? Why?' Fiona said, her annoyance rising a little. 'But anyway, why's your mum calling me and not you about this? I'm supposed to organise your whole life as well as my own because I'm a girl, I suppose?'

'No!' This unfairness stung him.

'Well why then?'

He was trapped. He looked at the footpath and his trainers. He could smell his feet. He wondered if other people could smell him, if dishonesty seeped from your skin, like those cancer smells that dogs could detect. They licked at patches on legs or arms, in places where tumours sprouted into being beneath the skin. He could say, I don't know what's happening to me. Or, I saw some animals, tortured. He saw Skye's pallor, her broken head.

'I just ran over somebody,' he said, his voice going into a high whisper. 'In the car.'

'*What?*' Fiona's irritation vanished. 'Oh, Stephen! Are you okay?'

'I just left her at a doctor's. But she landed on her *head*.'

He was tearful, grew more so with Fiona's sympathy. She said 'Oh, *honey*,' said *poor thing,* and he wished she were here now with her long arms about his neck, the soothing strength of her fingers over his shoulders. Whatever had to be done, all he wanted in this moment was her touch. At the thought of it he had to stop himself from letting out a sob, from telling her everything.

She had once told him that as soon as you placed your hands upon a stranger, they began to talk. Everybody found it so, she said: hairdressers, nurses, nuns. It was dangerously easy to give in: human defences dissolved at another person's touch.

A man in a tightly wound black turban stood on the pavement at the corner, waiting for the lights to change. From each of his hands hung a heavy plastic shopping bag, and he had a bus ticket stuck between his teeth. He tapped his foot, looking up the street towards an approaching bus.

At last Stephen said, 'I got Ella a ticket to the circus.'

'Did you,' Fiona said, deciding not to demur, demanding nothing from him. Having mercy. These old-fashioned words came to him. Clemency. Honour. Who was he to disavow such things?

Disavow? He was going mad. This must be shock. The bus loomed; the Sikh man tilted to cross the road. Stephen let out a long breath and gathered himself. He would leave the car, catch the bus. He would regain control of this day, get a grip. He would do what must be done.

Fiona began to speak, but Stephen knew he must stop this. He hardened his voice. 'I have to go.'

He pushed the phone into his pocket, hurried across the road with the Sikh man and climbed on to the bus.

He found an empty double seat towards the back and slid into it, rested his head against the window.

As the bus filled with people he saw a black-and-white dog tied by its lead to one of the bus shelter's supporting posts. Nobody seemed to own the dog. It sat, feet and tail neatly tucked away, mouth open and tongue hanging in the heat, patiently waiting. Stephen's hands rested in his lap, astonishingly still. A ghostly body was there inside his own, quaking and shivering, but outwardly his hands did not tremble. He was in shock. He had run over someone and it was not his fault. Or it was his fault, and she would die. Hit and run. Is this what they meant? He had hit someone, and now he was running.

Just below his eye level, taped to the bus-shelter's pole, was a flyer (the city was full of flyers—nobody knew anybody; if you wanted human contact you had to put a sign up in the street and summon strangers). This one was for the Norton Laughing Club. Stephen almost burst into scornful laughter himself as he read: *Need some chuckles in your life? Come join us each Friday, Dunmore Park.* There was a phone number to call. Stephen had heard of this: people stood round in a circle, practising different kinds of laughing. In public. Who were these sad fuckers who needed to go to a club once a week to manufacture laughter? It was the most depressing thing he had ever heard.

The bus moved off, and the tethered dog looked at the ground, waited in the grimy heat. It thought whoever had abandoned it was coming back.

In front of Stephen sat a muscle-bound young man who might be Lebanese, the curls of his hair shaved away on both sides of his head, turning the squared-off crown into a thick black mat. Across the back of the boy's black t-shirt was printed HARDEN THE FUCK UP in white military-style stencilled capitals. The squared head and rounded shoulders made Stephen think of the hippopotamus at the zoo. People thought hippos were cute, until they saw one. He imagined the boy's aggressive round nostrils, the small malevolent eyes, the gleaming flesh of his face. An old man sat beside the boy and Stephen could see hair coming from his ears beneath the band of a bright yellow baseball cap embroidered with *Snoop Dogg* in black graffiti-style lettering. It passed through Stephen's mind to wonder if his own father had had ear-hair like that before he died. He hoped not. The baseball cap was embarrassing, but

Stephen was too overcome to care. The air in the bus was stifling, despite the rattle of the air-conditioning. He felt sweat between his shoulder-blades; he leaned his head against the window and half-closed his eyes.

The Sikh man sat at the very front of the bus, on the seat where you were supposed to let old people sit. Stephen tried not to watch old people getting on at each stop, and their dithering. He could not bear the tension, waiting to see if they would find a seat before the bus took off. Each one, once they reached their seat, had an expression of triumph. But nowadays the bus driver had to watch them in his mirrors like a hawk. The drivers were not allowed to take off until all the oldies had sat down, ever since an old woman died when her head slammed into the floor of the aisle. But the old people seemed never to realise this, and would stand in the aisle, looking up and down the empty seats as if choosing something from a supermarket shelf, not understanding—or not caring—that the bus wouldn't move until they sat down. It usually infuriated him, but not today. He no longer cared how late he was. He was simply glad to sit, be transported by forces beyond his control. He stared out of the spotted, grimy window and saw the junkie girl flying through the air again, plummeting, smacking her skull—narrow, bony as a sheep's—on the bitumen. He felt a surging tide of nausea again. He should ring the clinic. He had left his number, but he doubted she would call him.

At Clare Street a woman got on, dressed in spotless white: tight white jeans, white t-shirt with a picture of what looked like a peacock picked out in sequins. White boots. Her long ringleted hair, a dull, tired red, reached to her shoulders. When she turned, Stephen saw with a shock of embarrassment that she was old, must be at least seventy, beneath all the tight white clothes and make-up. She had a pink mobile telephone hanging from a patterned lanyard around her slouchy neck. Then he saw that the design on the lanyard was the repeated blob of the Sydney Olympics 2000 logo. The woman had kept the lanyard all this time. Probably she was a volunteer, one of that brigade of happy folk in brightly patterned short-sleeved shirts and their unblemished Akubra hats, pointing and ushering. Wearing their uniforms in the streets months after the games were over. Maybe the mobile phone cord was the only thing tying the woman in white to her glorious two weeks as an Olympic volunteer, standing beside a roped-off area, smiling fit to burst, motioning with her hands.

She climbed gingerly into a seat, settling her plastic bags around her.

He should have got the number of the clinic. This came to him in a bolt of urgency. Stephen twisted around in his seat, seized with panic. What if she died? He would be arrested for leaving the scene. For leaving her in the hands of a methadone nurse, for not insisting on the hospital. He pressed his face to the window, peering back along Queen Street. What was the street number of the clinic? There must be more than one methadone clinic in Norton. He had never noticed that one before; for all he knew there could be dozens of clinics in the long, colourless, grit-swept stretch of Queen Street.

The bus moved on. Just *calm bloody down*, Stephen told himself. It was his father's bellowed dictum on every holiday trip in the car when someone whined or screeched. Stephen would put the girl Skye from his mind. She had medical help. She was fine. The taxi driver was right, he thought bitterly. He should have left. He knew that was wrong, but allowed himself the surge of self-pity. He had done the right thing. He had done *more* than the right thing. Stephen tried out this way of thinking: she was only a junkie, after all. Stupid bloody junkie who had no right to scare the shit out of him like this. They all had death wishes. But Stephen did not have the heart for it; instead what kept coming to him was his mother and the television news, hand over mouth. Poor creature.

Near the intersection of Fitzroy and Swan streets he saw the yellow road-sign, REFUGE ISLAND. A replica of the signs of his childhood in Rundle, egg-yolk yellow with its thick black border, the stencilled image of the two figures, slightly bent as if in frail, unsteady movement. When Stephen was a kid there was a refuge island sign in the centre of Aurora Street as it stretched down to the town-centre, and the figures were boy-and-girl silhouettes. Back then, as a child, he associated the sign with the wailing people who populated the evening news—the Vietnamese refugees in their papery wooden boats, landing exhausted and frightened on Australia's shores. Boat People, they were called, and to his child's ears it seemed these might be pirate people, or somehow connected to the Owl and the Pussycat. But on the television there were no birds nor cats, only the howling children and stick-thin, ruined parents on the broken boats, and the concrete strip in Aurora Street became forever linked with them, an island for these wretched, half-dressed children.

The bus moved off again, but in Stephen's mind these images bundled and collapsed, folding over one another like the leaves of those origami paper fortune-tellers that children made. So that even seeing the sign here, outside an inner city row of terrace shops, he felt himself to be six years old, safe on Rundle's refuge island, one hand clutching the pole and the other reaching out to offer welcome and shelter to the poor, discarded wreckage of the heartless world's distant wars.

The bus had stopped for too long. Stephen looked up as a gaunt, dishevelled young man stood by the driver's side, searching his voluminous clothes for a ticket, calling too loudly to the driver *don't worry mate, I'm not gunna getcha in trouble.* The driver glanced warily at the man and then shoved at the gears, and the bus moved off. The man found his ticket and screwed it down into the machine, then swayed away, forgetting to take it out again. He teetered up the aisle with his arms out to either side to steady himself, searching the faces of the people in the seats closely, as if looking for someone he knew. Stephen felt the shimmer of anxiety fill the bus, saw all the people turn their faces from the man. His hair was shoulder-length, dyed jet black and matted, not quite dreadlocked, and he wore thick black-rimmed glasses.

There were no lenses in the frames. The people on the bus felt for their mobile phones and pretended to read text messages, or concentrated their gaze beyond the man, on the strip of advertisements above his head—ads for cold sore cream and airport novels and pictures of a suspicious package with the government's terrorism warnings. IF YOU SEE SOMETHING, SAY SOMETHING.

The man still wandered ominously up the aisle. His gaze, quick-moving, birdlike, swept the seats, and Stephen knew there was no vacant seat except the one beside him. He could smell the man now, as he approached, and he sighed silently. He narrowed his shoulders and shifted toward the window to make way as the man sat down heavily, his khaki clothes flapping, his wet lips moving. Stephen turned his face to the window to avoid the man's breath and any potentially insane conversation. The man inhaled and exhaled loudly through his nose, dragging in the air, forcing it out again. And now, as Stephen knew he would, he began to mutter low, emphatic declarations to himself, his voice a little slurred and the words running together. 'Bescountry on earth,' he whispered to his chest. He snickered, and whispered, 'Besfucking*city* on earth.'

Then he gave a low, private snort of disgust: '*Melbourne.* Gimmeabreak.'

Stephen stared out of the window again, stared so hard his eyes watered. This was the trouble with living in Norton. The place was full of fucking mad people. Like the man who used to wander past his bedroom window at four-thirty every morning, pushing a trolley from the Norton Village Plaza before him, jingling along the uneven council pavement in the dark. One morning, after a new couple had moved in across the lane and begun renovating, Stephen heard their window wrench open and the neighbour shout at the trolley man in his clear, educated voice: 'Piss off, you freak.' The trolley had stopped instantly. Stephen was not awake enough to get up and look out, but he imagined the man, stock-still and terrified, his private singing-trolley world suddenly torn open. He never came back after that, and Stephen sometimes imagined him now sitting in some horrid dark room, longing to be out with his trolley, too frightened to set off. He hoped he found another route.

Then there was the middle-aged woman with the lank, steel-coloured hair and the mammoth, cannon-shaped breasts that swung low and loose and frightening beneath the stretched cotton of her faded little-girl floral dresses, who sang her strange operatic callings directly in front of the glass sliding doors of the Plaza entrance, breaking a loaf of bread apart and throwing enormous chunks of it down to the Welcome To Our Norton Village Plaza doormat, so the mat covered instantly with ravenous pigeons. To get into the Plaza the shoppers had to walk around the woman, standing with her hands lovingly clasping her own body, her long mad hair falling. She was like that painting of Venus on the seashell, beaming, only her grin was inane and her shell was a doormat and a dirty sea of pigeons. Then the security guard would arrive on his Segway and bark at her to go away.

There were the other asylum-seekers too, drawn to the Plaza like moths to light: the small, shifty man who wore a woollen beanie no matter the weather, and walked as if climbing over some eternally reappearing obstacle. At all times he clutched a longneck of beer inside a wrinkled paper bag, but Stephen had never seen him open it or drink from it. Sometimes he sat on Stephen's front fence, smoothing the paper bag around the bottle. There was the wild-haired homeless man from this morning who came and went, making a little nest of his belongings at the foot of the Plaza wall across the road from Stephen's house. Once, in the middle of this last cold winter, Stephen had given him some money and an old blanket. He couldn't stand the idea of the man sleeping out there without any covering. The man had shrunk back, alert, as if he expected Stephen to kick or shout at him. He said *efkharisto*, taking the blanket warily. The next morning Stephen saw Nerida standing at the homeless man's empty nest, pouring a bucket of water into the little pile of his belongings. Nerida would feed a stray cat or fret if Balzac had a cough, but the homeless were as intolerable as vermin.

When he was young and first came to the city, this daily witnessing of insanity—and of cruelty—shocked Stephen, and frightened him. In Rundle, it seemed, madnesses and cruelties were private affairs, if they existed, but here in the city each day brought some public hostility; each day you saw one human being degraded by another. You got used to it. If it was not directed at you, you learned to cast your eyes down and walk on by. If it was, you did the same thing but faster.

On his first day in the city, living by the beach, Stephen walked out of his new share house to buy a newspaper and reeled as he saw a man next to a car, shouting at a woman. He had a fistful of her hair in his hand, and she was bent awkwardly over the car bonnet. Stephen gaped, forgetting his sister Mandy's first injunction for living in the city: don't make eye contact. He wondered if he should call the police, but then the man turned to him and snarled, 'What are you looking at, cunt?' and Stephen was so frightened he scurried back inside his house and shut the door. The last thing he saw was a child, sitting quietly in the back seat of the car.

Stephen never grew accustomed to it, the same way he never got used to the rain. A country boy grown up with drought-dust, whose lungs had never had to tolerate the smell of mildew, at thirty-nine he was still awed by the torrential rainstorms that dumped down upon the city, the days and days of rain, the skies staying dark day-long, the soft fur of mould growing over your leather shoes in your wardrobe. And he still flinched if he heard swearing in the street—even schoolgirls did it, shouting out 'fuck' and 'pussy' and other shocking things. Stephen had no problem with conversational swearing, but each time he heard a curse bellowed in the street he had to stop himself looking guiltily around, in case one of his mother's friends or the Rundle Rotary Club vice-president might hear.

But the worst thing you never got used to was this: the man beside him now leaned suddenly close, making Stephen shut his eyes. You never got used to being trapped into intimacy with the mad. He could smell the man's breath, and hear it. He desperately did not want to be taken into deranged, foul-smelling patriotic confidences about the best country on earth, to be forced to agree that New Zealanders were sheepfuckers, that Melbournians were wankers. He did not wish to be that person on the bus for whom every other passenger felt pity, but also gratitude, because it was not they who were being berated, breathed upon, wheedled at, humiliated. Stephen was the one to be pitied—but also judged for his coldness, his distaste, his craven fear of insanity.

Please don't talk to me, Stephen prayed, the vibrations of the bus's engine passing through the window pane into his skull, *please*-don't-talk-to-me, *please*-don't-talk-to-me, in the rhythm of the roughly idling motor. He felt the man lean away again, and when he snuck a furtive glance he saw he had shifted his weight not to get close to Stephen, but only to draw a magazine from one of his capacious pockets. He sat reading it now. It was called *Dominion* and had an astronaut in a space suit on the cover.

At the Burlington, the man got up and swung away down the aisle, shouldering other passengers out of his way. Stephen was swept with relief. He knew the man was harmless. They were all harmless. They scared the shit out of him.

Stephen flipped open the magazine left on the seat. Its opening pages were full of short, snidely righteous letters referring to 'so-called biology', attended by lots of biblical reference numbers. *I found your article 'How Did Dinosaurs Get so Big, and How Did Noah Fit Them on His Ark?' to raise some most interesting questions. It's time the so-called 'scientists' are called to account. Keep up the good work. (Ex. 20:2; Deut. 7:6).* One letter complained about militant evolutionists taking over classrooms and suppressing facts supporting the Bible. *We must be vigilant.* Stephen turned the magazine over and looked again at the cover. *Exposing the myths and lies of evolution*, said a subtitle. It cost $7.80. Someone had paid for this.

'Jesus Christ,' he muttered. He flipped to the middle. Photographs of the Japanese tsunami covered three pages—people running for their lives from the wall of brown water and travelling buildings; cities turned to piles of sticks; the bodies of dead children lain in rows in the mud. Under the headline, *Tsunami: We've Been Here Before*, someone called Turner Bartlett (an importer/exporter living in regional Victoria) reiterated the tsunami's devastation in cold scientific detail. There were seismologist's maps and geological diagrams of ocean earthquakes. Stephen scanned the paragraphs, trying to find the point. Then, far down in the article he found a subheading, *Unprecedented catastrophe?*

> No. Noah's Flood was seven-hundred-thousand times greater than the 2011 tsunami which caused so much destruction. Only Noah heeded the warnings God gave the populace, and only eight people—Noah and his family—survived. Many people in Japan died because they did not heed the warnings of the Bible. If they had only paid attention to Noah's story, they might still be alive today.

Stephen closed the magazine and dropped it to the floor. He looked around, hoping nobody had seen him reading it. While he had been absorbed in the magazine, the passengers had thinned out as the bus drew nearer to the harbour. The only people left were two girls who looked to be in their early twenties talking in a loud, actressy way; an old man way down the front whose hand kept rising to pick at a scab on the crown of his head; and a man of about forty wearing a cheap-looking grey suit, his gaze fixed on the mobile phone in his hand while the other lifted a paper coffee cup to his mouth. He lowered his lips to the plastic lid and clamped them softly over it like a kiss. The Lebanese boy and the old man had long gone, and a delicately built Asian girl now sat in the seat in front of Stephen, a textbook open on her lap. She was studying the structure of silica. Her long hair was shiny black, and very fine. Across the aisle from Stephen, a solid middle-aged woman who could be a worn-out mother of a teenager, or a youngish grandmother, stared absently out of the window.

His mother was not ill, he decided. She was only seventy-four. She was fit as a fiddle, she always said. She had arthritis in her hands, but that was normal. But still, the last time he was in Rundle Stephen had been shocked by the weakness of her grip. She spent the whole weekend handing him bottles to open and her kitchen drawers were full of objects to help perform the simplest tasks—opening jars, picking things up off the floor. She had little claw-grabber things on sticks, and ugly rippled rubber mats in the bathroom. Even, he saw, a horrible white plastic chair in the shower stall of her en suite. There was a tray of white plastic pill bottles and vitamin jars from the chemist on a corner of the kitchen bench, which she covered with a white lace doily. That was the worst of all. Stephen had found it distasteful and made a joke about it, told her the house was starting to look like a frigging nursing home. He sat on the bus now, his cheeks colouring at the memory of her offence, snapping at him that he didn't have to live there and could go back to the city whenever he pleased.

'I don't ask you for much,' she had said this morning. But it *was* too much. He wished he could properly eradicate her injured voice on the phone. He was so tired, already, of managing his mind, of fending off all the things that must not be allowed to burden him today.

It was a relief to eavesdrop on the arch, affected chatter of the two girls at the front of the bus. Not that he had to try. They spoke loudly, performed their conversation the way all young people on buses did. Not just girls, boys did it too, braying to one another at top volume about themselves, their friends. Exploits with alcohol and authority and money and coded references to sex were detailed with loud guttural laughs and swaggers throughout the city's public transport system. Had Stephen ever been like this? Had his sisters? He didn't think so, but youth was a long time ago. Perhaps he and his friends had preened and flexed and fidgeted, drawing attention to themselves in the way he saw hulking young men doing every day. Perhaps Mandy and Cathy had cursed and laughed and fingered their slender white throats and fondled their own hair in the way the two girls on the bus did now.

One of them—the peachy one, all firm roundness in her shoulders and cheeks and breasts—suddenly put her hand on her friend's arm and gasped.

'Oh my *God* I forgot to tell you.' She flicked her hair from her eyes in a coy, faux-apologetic way. 'There's a nudie picture of me on Facebook.'

The other girl, also pretty with long straight hair (did any woman under forty have short or curly hair?) considered her friend's dilemma for a microsecond. Then she shook herself, as if emerging from some quaint but pointless reverie. 'But that's fine!' she said. The first girl was instantly, stupidly at ease. 'Oh yeah! I thought it was, and then I didn't know. But cool!'

They went on to discuss how what the peachy one *really* wanted was a little jeans miniskirt.

Stephen thought of the nude photograph, trapping the compromised girl there on the internet forever; some blurred mobile phone image of her breasts or bum or opened thighs. Worse, her face as well, rich with desire. Would she ever again consider this exposure? Would Larry and Ella grow up to be like this: long-limbed and pale, shockingly confident, utterly unprotected? What would Fiona do, if one of the girls got carted to hospital to have her stomach pumped, or she found a pregnancy test in the bathroom rubbish bin?

No. He would not have it. This would not happen to Ella or Larry. They would not grow up to be handled— *photographed*—by men, they would not endanger themselves, cause Fiona heartache and sorrow. But he knew it would happen. And Fiona would be alone with it, all through the anxious small-hours sickening heartbreak of them not coming home. If she wasn't with another man, that was. But Stephen instantly closed the opening of that possibility, *snap*, and dropped it away into the far, far depths of his mind.

No. It would not be a man. It would be Fiona's old friends who would save her. The friends from before her marriage, from college—the other physiotherapists, speech pathologists, social workers, who met in their first years on the public hospital wards before they all grew tired of the shit pay and the hours and the abuse, and drifted off to start their own private practices.

Sometimes these friends still gathered noisily at Fiona's place for drinks and pretend book club, dumping tubs of hummus and a couple of paperbacks on the table, then breaking into affectionate chatter. When Fiona was with them, any guardedness in her disappeared.

She was all openness, all ruby iridescence, as she joined their shrieks and cackles, their adoration of each other. How unashamed they were, in their blithe appraisals and comparisons of each other's bodies, the exacting dissection of their emotions. They held each other's hands across couches, lavished compliments on one another's cooking, earrings, ankles, shoes. They exchanged health worker war stories, of fuckwit famous footballers with ankle injuries, or gruesome tales from people they knew who still worked on the wards.

Stephen busied himself with the girls in adjoining rooms and eavesdropped on the women, their conversation gothic and entrancing: 'The boyfriend yelled out, Anthony's hurt himself! So she ran in—but what he'd *actually* yelled was, Anthony's *hung* himself.'

He glimpsed them through doorways as they regaled each other with ghastly tales of accidents, of failed suicide attempts and their aftermath, speaking with relish as they plunged rice crackers into dips.

'I saw a guy once, terrible depression for years, shot himself like this'—one of the speech pathologists once said, a finger-gun beneath her chin—'but he aimed wrong. Completely missed the brain; it all came out here.' She held a hand vertical at her nose, let her fingers fall forward in an arc. 'His depression completely disappeared and he wanted to live. And I thought, oh darling, nobody's going to want you now.'

She took a cheerful swig of wine; the others nodded lazy grins. None of this was unfamiliar; they all had patching-up stories.

'And I'm supposed to get him talking again,' she said, 'but you know, where's the tongue?'

There was the blackest of laughter, and then through the doorway Stephen saw Fiona look up—or he sensed it first—to see where he was, to see if he had heard. Perhaps she made some signal to the others he could not see, to quieten their macabre turn of conversation.

Always he has met her eye steadily, through doorways, across rooms.

When a shocking thing happened to you, people—women, mostly—related your whole life to it; this is what Stephen had learned. They watched for it to spill out, for your suffering to show. They wanted it; they made little spaces for it to happen, were disappointed when it didn't. The reason Fiona looked around for him at such moments was that years ago, in Rundle, a man he'd known in passing shot himself and Stephen saw it happen. So did other people. It was horror, and it passed. But women liked to link you forever to that one thing. They loved it, made it become the pivot, the story, of your life. But the death, and even his own father's death soon afterwards (he had opened his eyes once, swept a potent gaze over his wife, his children around his bed, before he died), were not the story of Stephen's life. They were not his excuse. Because life went on. Fiona's friend's suicide story showed this, all their laughing at it showed it too. This is what he would say to Fiona, it came to him now: upsetting things happen, and you get through them, and life goes on. Fiona would be all right. The women would gather with sauvignon blanc and casseroles, and gradually begin to kick at the edges of Fiona's feeling for Stephen, heeling off little lumps of it like clumps of clay from a cliff edge. *I mean, he's sort of a nice guy and everything.* Letting her doubt it. *But what was he actually offering you?* And one day, quite soon, Fiona would sit back with a start and find she could not recall his face very well, and wonder what had possessed her to fall in love with him.

At the zoo there were therapy classes for arachno-phobes, where they made people hold great monstrous spiders in the palms of their hands. Stephen had seen it, watching from the back of the room one day during his lunch break. People all over the place, tears streaming down their faces, and in the centre of their open, shaking palms the terrible black spiders squatted, crumpled black pipe cleaner legs as thick as human fingers. Why a person would do this to herself Stephen had no fucking idea. But there you were. People got over all sorts of things.

The woman across the aisle turned from the window and caught his eye before turning away again, expressionless. Stephen wondered briefly what her glance at him told her, but he didn't really want to know.

Just then Stephen noticed something on the floor under one of the bus seats, between the woman and the man with the phone. He bent his head to see it. It was a silver plastic bag, oddly shaped as if the bag had been wrapped around something. It was shoved up against the pole of a seat, on the dirty lino floor. He could see part of a shop logo printed on the bag, a swirling pink *Gi* of what must, in those colours, say '*girl*'.

A high tinnitus whine of alarm started up deep inside Stephen's ears.

Someone had just left it there accidentally, obviously. Some shopping bag left behind. But the bag was not new. The silver was scuffed, wearing off here and there to reveal the white plastic beneath. And it was wrapped tightly around the thing inside it. The thing had not been slipped in by a shop assistant's manicured hand and handed over with a smile. Someone had shoved the thing, the rounded heavy thing—heavy enough for it not to slide around with the motion of the bus—into the bag and left it there, and got off the bus.

If you see something, say something.

Stephen looked around at the people, willing someone to catch his eye. But nobody did. Nobody looked in his direction.

He grasped hold of his own hands. This was ridiculous. It had been a terrible morning. The junkie girl, sailing above the traffic, a sallow malnourished angel. Then the sickening plummet. He wondered where she was now. Perhaps she had gotten herself home on the glazed momentum of the methadone, and sat down on the couch, where the leaking vein inside her brain, allowing the slow seep of blood all through the spongy coral, could no longer withstand the pressure. It suddenly tore and burst and she, the junkie girl Skye whom he had hit with his car, cried out in anguish and clutched her head, and died, all alone on her dingy couch.

He breathed out. In and out. *In*, hold, and *out*, the way he had learned from yoga Dawnelle.

The bus heaved off from a stop where nobody got on or off. Stephen looked again at the silver bag. Now he had seen it, it glowed there beneath the seat. He could not believe nobody else had noticed it. For if they did, surely someone would raise the alarm. Stephen did not know what bombs looked like. Could they be bulky like this? Surely these days all they needed was a mobile phone, some small electronic wizardry they could detonate remotely. But, he reasoned, the thing had to be big to contain enough explosives to do the damage. As big as a bucket? Have to be. And the bag was much smaller than a bucket. Half a bucket, probably.

But the thrumming in his ears grew louder, despite his reasoning, and his heartbeat began to match it. Breathing was not helping, and in fact he began to feel a little lightheaded. Would they know, when it went off, that it was happening—or would it be so big, so instant, that all you would know was a burst in your eardrums, and then black? That wouldn't be so bad, would it?

For one shameful second he was liberated: if a bomb went off he would not have to tell Fiona.

But then he recalled the photographs of the London bombings—people staggering around covered in blood.

That girl with no legs, who went on television. People with their arms blown off, but still alive, still conscious.

The bag seemed to pulse there now, against the iron leg of the seat.

Stephen's head ached, his body was soaking in sweat, now his guts churned and it was only ten o'clock in the morning. There could be a bomb.

He missed his father. He hated this city.

He imagined his mother's morning in Rundle, what she would be doing now. Folding the tennis newsletter into envelopes, perhaps, licking and sticking. Or clipping greenery from the garden if it was her turn to do the flowers for Mass. He envied the pure simplicity of Rundle life, where there were no bombs on buses—there were no buses. No junkies ran into traffic in Rundle, images of tortured creatures were not thrust at you as soon as you left your house. There were no workplace teambuilding exercises to be endured, for there was no-one to run them.

The woman across the aisle had opened a tabloid newspaper. Stephen could see almost a full-page photograph of a hunted-looking dog behind the bars of a police wagon, its eyes large and glossy. VICIOUS ATTACK. It was the Rottweiler that had killed a child the day before in an outer suburb, savaging it while the parents were outside chatting to a neighbour. The dog was to be destroyed. Stephen imagined what the parents had found. The blood, the dog standing there, its four feet planted on the carpet, slavering over the motionless child. Waiting, wild-eyed and lost. He looked at the photograph, at the dog's bewildered eyes behind the bars. It had no idea what it had done.

Stephen looked out of the window again, thinking of the other dog in the news, the bomb-sniffing army dog that had been lost and then found in Afghanistan. Earlier in the week it was presented with a bravery award. It had been the good-news story at the end of all the television bulletins. There was a garden ceremony, with chairs and officials and speeches. The woman from the RSPCA had hung the Purple Heart around the dog's neck—it was only the second animal to get the medal after Simpson's donkey—and thanked the dog for its resilience and its *unquestioning service* to our troops. Although he had been alone in the room, Stephen had thrown back his head, looked about him for confirmation. Was this actually what the woman had said? And was he the only person to think a bravery medal for a dog was madness? The people at the ceremony clapped and looked tearfully moved. The newsreaders did too. Only Stephen and the dog, it seemed, were baffled. Everyone else seemed to think it perfectly normal to lead donkeys and dogs onto battlefields and then pretend they chose it for themselves, fired by patriotic valour.

Stephen's glance was dragged back to the bag beneath the seat. There were only three stops until this bus reached the interchange. He just needed to calm fucking down.

He pushed his mind back to Rundle where there were no bombs, where children were not killed by dogs or de factos, where no homeless people slept in nests of garbage. The streets were wide and flat, the empty skies enormous. Perhaps he would go and stay with his mother for a while. He could get a farm-hand job. There were farms where chickens ran free, and eggs were found in hiding places, not factories. It was romantic, but it comforted him. He could work somewhere out there, somewhere in the wide space and open air. Other people did this, didn't they?

The woman turned the newspaper and on the raised right-hand page a quote in enlarged type caught his eye: *'I work in people's gardens to earn money for food. Sometimes I collect firewood and sell it.'* That was the kind of thing, exactly. It was an omen. He could do that. He saw himself in his ute, gardening tools sliding round the back, an axe for chopping wood. He felt his heartbeat slowing. It was clear to him now. He could lift himself out of this miserable city, this complicated, messed-up life. He could build a wooden hut on someone's bush block, greet each day with the birds, a cup of tea steaming in his hands. Jane Doepel from his high school was running an organic cashew farm outside Rundle now, his mother had told him. He remembered Jane Doepel's long, lithe legs at the year ten athletics carnival. He could work for her, build his hut on her place. Grow his own vegetables and barter them for meat. He knew he was being crazy now, but for the first time today Stephen felt a clearing, an opening out of something good and pure. People did these things, didn't they? It wasn't beyond the realm of possibility. People changed their lives all the time. Wasn't it this, in fact—free will, the ability to determine one's own path in life—which separated humans from the beasts?

The woman folded her newspaper, and as she did he saw the lower half of the page. The person quoted about the gardening and the firewood was a starving woman from Darfur. It was an ad for third world aid.

He turned away. The fucking bag was still there, still monstrously present, still unnoticed by anyone but him. He stared out of the window, willing himself not to look at it. Then it came to him, a sudden, welcome slosh of cold water. Someone's gym shoes. That was it! A smelly pair of gym shoes, taken off before going into the office. Relief flooded through him.

But when he looked again the parcel did not have the shape of shoes. It was too high, too round. *If you see something, say something.* Seconds passed. Stephen found his fingers pressing the stop button, found he had leapt to his feet and was stepping fast down through the flung-open back doors of the bus.

He stood, panting, on the pavement as the bus moved away.

The woman with the newspaper, the cheap suit, the Asian student, the old man with the scabbed head, the driver and the actressy Facebook girls, all unaware, all trapped there in the bus with the throbbing silver bundle that may be a lunch box or a jumper or a pair of gym shoes or a home-made peroxide-based explosive device.

Stephen had seen something and said nothing, and he heard the thrum of his cowardice in his ears long after the bus disappeared from view.

In his pocket his phone vibrated. He looked at the screen, saw CATHY MOBILE. He considered it there in his hand, shivering its long, accusing notes. He imagined her at work at the pharmacy, standing before the white shelves of pills in the dispensary, waiting for him to answer. Biting her lip in rage. He knew how her voice would sound, and that he had not the strength to hear it. The phone stopped vibrating. He breathed out. In a moment a message flashed up: *Call me.*

CHAPTER 3

As Stephen hurried through the zoo entrance, the crisp, amplified voice of a woman came to him through the birdcalls and the rustle of eucalypts high above, her schoolteacher's voice rising and sinking on the currents of the air.

It was ten-thirty. He was supposed to be here an hour ago. Stephen put his head down and pushed up the path, trying to breathe deeply. It was even hotter now, the sun very high in the swollen blue sky, and he was faintly dizzy with exertion. He wiped his face; if he could only find an edge of this fine mask of perspiration, lift and peel it away, he would feel better. His feet burned in his sneakers; they were laced too tight, pressing painfully on the top of his feet. All he could think now, apart from praying that Mia was not already looking for him, was of wrenching off his shoes, plunging his feet in cold water.

He almost looked forward to the punishment of the deep fryer now. The other things—his mother, the junkie girl's internal bleeding, his dread about this afternoon—could be allayed for a while by the simple, visceral hatred he had for this job. The shining golden swing of the oil as he turned the valve, the rude fishy stench as it slubbed and glugged, the slippery art of holding the mouth of the tin in place, then once all the old oil was gone and the boil-out done, the ache that would spread up his back as he hung over the edge into the great rancid space of the ancient fryer, scrubbing its walls, the skin of his fingers puckering in the sweaty rubber gloves. You couldn't clean the oil entirely from your skin—it just had to wear off over days, as did the metallic stink his hair would take on despite the hygiene cap.

We're pretty famous for our snakes in Australia, the voice said through the trees.

Ahead of him on the curving grey footpath a man in a dun-coloured zookeeper's uniform carried a bucket in one hand and a bicycle wheel in the other. The animal attendants were always walking around carrying things. Sacks, buckets, armfuls of branches—but also weird things like this: bicycle parts, or huge pieces of brightly coloured polystyrene foam. You rarely actually saw these people inside the cages—*exhibits*, they were not allowed to call them cages—and it seemed to Stephen they simply mooched about all day carrying these odd combinations of objects. As long as you wore a pair of khaki pants you could pretty much get away with anything here. How many strange combinations of objects would you have to walk round clutching before someone questioned you? A bag of muesli and an umbrella? A violin bow and a chainsaw? As long as you had that purposeful stride, nobody would bat an eyelid.

The Bush Clearing came into view. Stephen could see, through the gaps in the deliberately rustic fence posts, a few people scattered on low benches around the shallow amphitheatre, all eyes intent on the woman standing down on the grass before them with her arms outstretched. She squinted up at the people and flicked her high black ponytail as she spoke, her voice amplified by the kind of headset microphone worn by motivational speakers or stadium evangelists. Through and around her outstretched arms, a huge snake slowly curled and slithered. The woman's name was Melanie, she told the audience, and she was a snake handler here at the zoo.

'I s'pose we should be famous, 'cos we do have some of the deadliest snakes in the world,' Melanie said cheerfully, too loudly, into the microphone bud. She wore a green zoo windcheater, khaki shorts and workman's boots. She began strolling through the crowd, the enormous splotch-patterned snake swaying in her arms. It looked heavy. Stephen watched the clutches of people draw back from Melanie and the snake as she walked; nervous laughter and flutters of whispered Japanese and German rose up from the crowd.

'But we also have some beautiful and gentle snakes, like this *gorgeous* diamond python,' shouted Melanie. She rotated one of her shoulders and her wrist, twisting the snake's face to meet hers. She smiled lovingly at it. Stephen half expected her to kiss its deadly looking mouth, as if she were a bride, festooned and looped and draped with black-and-yellow-patterned snake.

'And this python's name is—' said Melanie, and then stopped, puzzled.

She turned to look over her shoulder towards the other snake handler standing behind her on the grass, bored as a security guard. Legs apart, hands behind his back, a canvas sack pooled open at his feet. 'Which one's this, again?' Melanie whispered to him, loud and clear into the mike.

The other man shrugged. It was of no interest to him.

Melanie turned back to peer at the python again for a moment, her face blank. Then she took charge. 'Wirri Gurri,' she said in a firm voice, beaming at the audience. The other handler stared.

'Which, in our local *indigenous* language, means,' said Melanie, looking around, then casting her gaze upwards, 'Very Big Tree.'

A satisfied murmur moved through the crowd. Melanie, back on familiar ground now, resumed her stroll through the benches, lowering the python into people's faces. 'Have a pat, she's *lovely*.'

Melanie's voice followed Stephen through the trees. 'Go on, she feels beautiful. Nah, go on. She won't hurtcha.'

The lorikeets squealed and shrieked as Stephen passed the bilby-and-bat house, the Crocodile Crepes Cafe sandwich board chained to a light pole. He could feel the sun burning his scalp through his hair.

You right? Melanie's voice was still cheerful, but with a little note of irritation.

The lurid orange Goodfellow's tree-kangaroo sat on its ugly bare branch, surveying him with a level gaze as he passed. Stephen had always felt unnerved by it: that musty colour, its voley face. He was glad of the fence. He looked down at the bitumen as he walked, passing a woman crouched behind a pram, scrabbling into its basket underneath, while all around her on the footpath was strewn the detritus of early childhood—bottles, several plastic bags, a purple lunch box, two nappies.

Melanie, still audible, sounded disconcerted now. *Oh. Are you her husband? She'll be all right in a minute, I reckon.* There was a note of steel in her voice, and now a loud shuffling, a laboured breathing noise as Melanie's headset moved and rubbed against something. Then, as if struck by a thought, her voice asked the high blue air over the city, *Actually, is anyone else actually really scared of snakes?* There was a moment's pause before her equanimity returned. *I should of asked that before, I s'pose.* And her high, microphoned giggle floated through the trees.

The Caribbean flamingos teetered on their folding crimson legs, clucking and squawking, their beaks at the end of the snaking, pink-stockinged necks inscribing arcs on the muddy water. A sign nearby claimed the flamingos did not fly away because they were very content in their exhibit, and also because one wing had been pinioned in a painless surgical procedure carried out under general anaesthetic, after which they showed no desire to fly.

He passed the barren, stony enclosure for the Barbary sheep. There were no sheep to be seen, but there was a swishing noise, and high up on a ledge a keeper moved, patiently sweeping the rocks with a straw broom, the black walkie-talkie at his belt jiggling as he moved. The sheep, Stephen saw then, were huddled down at the fence line, heads in a trough.

At the Sumatran rhino enclosure the line for the next session was growing. Ever since the rhino calf was born it was the zoo's star attraction, and staggered viewing-times had to be introduced. The birth—only the second in captivity—was covered on the television news and the commercial channels named the infant Mr Waddles. Its official name was Adik, apparently a term of endearment translating as 'little brother', but nobody called it that.

Stephen watched the queue as he drew near. At the end of the line two large women stood shifting their weight uncomfortably in the blazing heat. Between them a boy of nine or ten slouched on the low ledge of the garden bed, and the women—one in a leopard-print, one in a zebra-striped top pulled down over her shorts—looked down at him, discussing him as if he were an exhibit himself. 'He's sick of the band-aid, he says it's getting itchy,' one of the women said. She reached down and turned the boy's head, using his ear as a handle, to show her friend a band-aid behind his ear. The friend murmured in reply, keeping her arms folded in a repelled way. She kept her hands to herself. The boy, listless and bored, did not speak. He did not look well.

The women fanned themselves with zoo maps and pulled at their clothes. The first reached beneath one armpit, pinching the stretchy zebra-print fabric away from her body to cool herself. Stephen imagined the body odour on her fingers. 'This thing better be good,' she said, straining to look at the line ahead, to see if anyone was moving. Beside them was a sandwich board advertising the Rhino Shop that stood not far from the enclosure, a separate demountable room selling rhino merchandise. There were rhino cups, rhino slippers, rhino computer mouse pads, rhino-shaped chocolates, stuffed fluffy rhino toys (mother and baby joined by an elastic strap), rhino doorstoppers, mobile phone covers, rulers, pens, notepads and key rings. At first there had been rhino-foot umbrella-holders made of plastic for $59.99, but these had been removed after some complaint, and the zoo acknowledged that there had been an error of judgement in the merchandise ordering and that the umbrella-holders had sent the wrong message.

On a wall outside the enclosure was a photograph each of Adik and his mother Long-Long. In the rhino merchandise the animals were made to look appealing in a cuddly, big-horned way, but in the flesh there was no way round it: they were hideous. Their heads were boot-shaped and elongated, concave where they should have bulged and blunt where they should have had points. Their stumpy legs were too short for the great bodies, they had bizarrely shaggy hides and lashless, bulging eyes. Adik didn't even have a horn, just a tumorous swelling on his snout. As if to compensate for this repulsive alienness, the photographs were accompanied by paragraphs about the creatures' inner lives. *Adik: Born: 23/8/2011—Personality: Cute and pretty laid-back, can be very cheeky. Likes: His keeper Rusty; Bamboo Back Scratches. Dislikes: Getting out of bed on winter mornings!* Long-Long's personality, the sign said, was *pretty outgoing* and she liked *Rhino treats*.

Russell often threatened to poster some other information over the sign (*Dislikes: Being imprisoned against her will, Anthropomorphism*) but so far the only graffiti was the weekly scrawled misspelling of Adik's name, with accompanying drawings. A man with a squirty bottle of cleaner came to remove these after every school visit.

A little further on, just outside the rhino exit, two young women stood peering down, scrolling through photographs one had taken on her mobile phone. 'That was pretty lame,' one said. The other nodded, frowning, puzzled, at the pictures. 'It just sort of *stood* there,' she said.

The sun beat down.

Russell looked towards the Komodo dragon's enclosure as he dragged on his cigarette, eyes narrowed against the smoke. Smoking was prohibited within the zoo, but Russell paid no heed to the signs, nor the repeated warnings from Marilyn Parris, the catering director. The dragon was unvisited for a change, and it lay like a long, irregular stone against the wall of its house.

Russell was forty-three, had never married and lived alone in a rented one-bedroom flat in a distant suburb.

He didn't have a car, nor a mobile phone. He said the only topic of conversation more boring than real estate was mobile phones, and if anyone in his earshot said the word 'iPhone' Russell would leap to his feet, stick his fingers in his ears and begin screaming as if stabbed. Russell had a long-term girlfriend called Lucy who worked for customs, rummaging through people's suitcases at the airport, and who appeared to demand nothing more of him than weekends of television and cheerful sex. He was well read, knew a lot about history, made off-colour remarks about women and despised almost everyone. He abhorred ambition of any kind and had for years refused promotions or other enticements to remove him from contact with the zoo's public. Nobody knew how long he had worked at the kiosk, but his tenure originated in some ancient contract that made it impossible to shift him, and too expensive to pay off with a redundancy. The kiosk was his realm and he ran it how he wanted, employing shiftless men and women who could hold a drink and would laugh at his jokes. Russell kept a running tab on the decline of civilisation, documenting travesties in an exercise book he kept in the drinks fridge. *Item no. 2876: The word 'Awesome'.* Reality television had a whole section to itself. *Item no. 6759: 'Bondi Vet'.* He did not use the internet, had no intention of ever owning property and would never give up smoking. Russell watched nuclear families lining up outside the baboon house and nudged Stephen behind the counter. 'Look at this poor sad fucker, mortgaged up to his arsehole,' he would say, pointing his spatula across the piazza to where an overweight, weary-looking 32-year-old wearing the corporate dad's leisure uniform of navy cargo shorts, leather flipflops, aviator sunglasses and an *Andersen Consulting Fun Run 2009* t-shirt. Russell would yell, 'Might as well get inside the cage yourself, mate,' and turn back to the hotplate. Casually, as if the man had heard nothing, he would slowly turn around. Finding no culprit he would have to pretend serious interest in the plaque about the natural habitats of baboons. In the gloom of the kiosk Russell and Stephen would snigger happily and go on flipping burgers.

When Stephen saw Russell now, lazing at the outdoor table smoking a cigarette, a surge of gratitude flooded through him. Russell was his sane, intelligent, uncompromising friend. He slumped down on the bench beside him. 'Sorry I'm so bloody late.'

Russell kept gazing at the Komodo dragon, appearing not to have heard. He stretched out a skinny leg and leaned backwards on his metal stool to insert the cigarette lighter into his jeans pocket. 'I gave it a roll-mop the other day,' he said, staring wistfully at the beast. 'But it sicked it up.' The lighter now in place, he realigned himself to hunch once more over the table.

A woman and her elderly mother appeared at the dragon enclosure and stood, an empty stroller between them, at the fence. They had not noticed the huge concrete-coloured reptile merging into the wall; they were reading the sign. A little girl aged about seven, wearing an Australian flag cap and jeans, and a pink and yellow t-shirt that said *OMG!* on the front and *WTF!* on the back in large letters, eventually stomped up behind them, arms folded.

The mother suddenly noticed the dragon, gasped, and wheeled around to her child.

'*Look*, Bronte!' She crouched at her daughter's side, and pointed. 'Look at him. He can see you!'

Stephen had always found this strange, watching people at the zoo; their odd, desperate need for the animals to notice them. He's looking at us! He's coming over! Surely the most appealing thing about animals was that—far from offering unconditional love—they wanted nothing from you. He liked this absence from their comprehension—the fact that he could stand in front of the open eyes of the

Komodo dragon for an hour or a day or a week, and the dragon would apparently never register his presence, nor care. It was a chance for you to stop existing.

Overhead came the mingled sound of an aeroplane and the birds. One birdcall high, far away and whooping, rhythmic as a car alarm; others squirting in arrhythmic shrieks, squeaking discordant arcs, like rusted metal wheels turning. One rhythm overlapped another, dissolving in and out, the sounds of the zoo rising and sinking away.

The woman at the dragon enclosure gripped her daughter around the waist. 'See?' She cried. 'He's looking at you!'

Russell followed Stephen's gaze. 'Pathetic, isn't it.'

Bronte squirmed, pinned between her mother's body and the sharp edge of the fence. But the mother was undeterred, desperate for the dragon to show a sign of life. She shrieked now into the child's ear, 'He's watching us!'

Humans *were* pathetic, it was true. Stephen had left a busload of people for dead because he was too gutless to speak. But it wasn't only cowardice that had caused him to abandon them. It was something else. It was his knowledge of what would have happened if he raised the alarm—the irritated glances, the shrugs of disdain.

Some of them might casually get off at the next stop as if they had always planned it, but they would not thank him, nor show any fright. And some, out of a fear of looking panicked or stupid, would simply stay in their seats, riding to their deaths. Perhaps this was what separated us from the animals—not language, but embarrassment.

Although, Stephen thought as he and Russell watched the woman gripping her struggling daughter at the fence, prattling on, there were still quite a lot of people unencumbered by the problem of embarrassment.

'I saw a bunch of Yanks this morning, at the Eastern greys,' Russell said, tossing his cigarette butt to the concrete and twisting his heel over it, 'with their backs turned to the roos, videoing their kids. Hopping.'

A birdcall scratched at the air with a high, abandoned cry. *Hierk, hierk, hierk.*

'I gotta have a slash,' Russell said, getting up from his seat. 'Big Bertha's waiting for you.' He meant the fryer. Russell called everything by women's names.

Stephen wanted to tell Russell about the accident, about the junkie girl dying on her couch, about the bomb on the bus, about Fiona. But he was out of breath from the walk up the hill. And what would he say? He was exhausted, he was *hot*, and there was still the rest of the day to be endured.

The woman and her mother and the child wandered away from the dragon into the reptile house.

Hierk, hierk.

This was what he would tell Fiona. Things happen, they pass. Life casts you, you drift. He nodded as this occurred to him. You go with the flow. Animals and children understood this: everything was temporary. He was not running, not evading things; he was accepting the way of the universe. All things passed. He let a peaceful, Buddhist sort of feeling rise up in him. He could say these things, for they were true, he believed them. He could do it. He imagined looking into Fiona's eyes, and holding her hand, and saying these things. Then he felt sick.

For three hours he scrubbed at the slimy walls of the fryer. It was the fifth time he had done this job—they took it in turns—and it was the fifth time he wished they had changed the oil when they were supposed to. The oil was verging on rancid and the smell made him gag.

It was no cooler inside the kiosk than out, despite the whirring fans, and he had to use near boiling water in the buckets to cut through the film of grease. He was certain his body temperature had never been this high in his life; he was faint with it. The scouring pad soon grew slick with grease, and he found he was just shifting the oil from one part of the wall to another. Every so often he had to step outside the kitchen and stand in the trees with his hands on his knees, taking in great gulps of clean air. People passing with their children stopped to stare at him, the limp white hygiene cap drooping round his ears, the sweat pouring down his bright red face. He went back inside and scoured and scoured, the muscles of his arms and shoulders and his back burning. It was weird how, bent down into the vat, scrubbing, this greasy duty somehow kept reminding him of the interminable hours at Mass as a boy. Kneeling on the hard floor. Penance. He squeezed the scourer into the bucket and began again. Whenever his mother came to his mind, or Fiona, he scrubbed harder, as if he could rasp away what he had done, what he was yet to do.

After three hours he was finished. He was drenched in sweat, and still between his fingers and in the crooks of his elbows he felt the oil, no matter how many times he washed. His pants were wet with sweat and filth, and he remembered with a dull thump that in his hurry this morning he had not packed a change of clothes to wear at the birthday party.

Russell sat down beside him in the shade of one of the umbrellas, holding out a lemonade Icy Pole. Stephen unpeeled the sticky paper and sucked at the glorious cold ice.

'You look like shit,' Russell said. He nodded. He felt like shit.

Mia, assistant to the catering director, came strutting over the paving towards them in her sturdy high heels. She clutched a yellow A4 envelope in her right hand, and pressed her glossed lips together as she walked. She wore tiny tailored navy-blue shorts and a white top with thin shoulder straps, and her impressively sized breasts bounced behind each step. Despite these, and the appeal of those long tanned legs, Mia always made Stephen think of a praying mantis. The long triangular shape of her face, the blunt fringe making her eyes seem wider apart than was natural in a human face. Nevertheless Stephen and Russell watched her walking, appraising her as she approached. Russell said, 'Greetings, Torpedo Girl,' referring to her nipples, just as she reached them.

Mia could tell Russell had meant something vulgar, and eyed him as she thrust the envelope at Stephen. 'What's that smell?' she said, wincing in distaste.

'Hi, Mia,' Stephen said, 'I had to clean out the deep fryer. It's probably me. Sorry about that.'

Mia did not reply, but scowled past him to the koala enclosure, where a mother held a toddler up above the fence. 'Look, Karma,' the woman was calling. 'He's saying hello to you!'

The baby sucked its fingers.

'She should be paying for that,' Mia said, as she watched the woman clutch the baby to herself and scoot inside the unlocked gate. The enclosure was usually staffed by cheerful zoo employees who took photos of the kids next to a comatose koala and sold them to the parents for twenty-five dollars. But now there were no keepers to be seen, and the woman took her child right up to the koala.

Stephen dipped a hand into the envelope, feeling around for the one remaining piece of folded paper inside. Mia leaned back a little, as if afraid Stephen's hand might accidentally touch her own.

Stephen and Mia had bad blood over the catering division Kris Kringle since the previous year. He had drawn her name last year and then forgotten about it until the morning of the division's Kris Kringle Secret Santa Breakfast, when he suddenly remembered. He had no choice but to nip over to the supermarket in the Plaza in the early morning before work. He found a stainless steel insulated mug with a black plastic lid in the kitchenware section and wrapped it in generic birthday paper in the car at the traffic lights.

This was before Marilyn Parris arrived, when the director of catering was Sandy Box ('don't fuck with her,' Russell used to sing under his breath whenever she approached). Sandy was one of those bosses who liked to think of staff as her 'family' until she fired them or, by repeatedly cutting their budgets and raising the stakes on their key performance indicators, made their lives so intolerable they left. On the morning of the breakfast Sandy shouted, 'I'll be Santa!' and sat at the meeting room table, handing out the presents, squealing with fake laughter while the staff gravitated to the edges of the room, leaning with their backs against the windowsills, slowly chewing ham and cheese croissants.

Mia was first to receive her gift. When she unwrapped the cup she held it dangling from the crook of her index finger, as if trying to touch the least surface area possible, and looked around at her colleagues with open disgust. 'Who got me this?'

Stephen pretended not to hear, and Sandy's flouncing and screeching continued. Later, when it was safe, he glanced Mia's way and said casually, 'So what did Santa bring you, Mia?'

She turned to him, her face full of contempt. She lifted the cup in the air, let it hang. '*This.*'

Stephen said, 'Huh, wow,' with a small laugh, hoping it sounded sarcastic. He looked around as if to laugh at whoever might have bought it. Mia stared at him. 'Did *you* get me this?'

'God no,' Stephen had laughed, trying to emulate her disgust, and then leaned forward, as casually as he could, to reach for another croissant. 'God no,' he said again through his mouthful, and turned to raise his eyebrows in camaraderie as Jim, a large rumpled man who had something to do with payroll that Stephen never understood, sniggered uncontrollably while Jason from the Crocodile Crepe Cafe unwrapped a large pink dildo.

'Thanks, you prick,' Jason said quietly to Jim, smiling. Jason was gay. Stephen couldn't tell whether he was pleased or angry at the gift, but Jim kept chortling.

Stephen said, 'How do you know it's from Jim? It's supposed to be Secret Santa.'

They all grinned at him—even Jason grinned—as if he was stupid.

Mia kept a careful watch on the others as they opened their gifts. And to Stephen's growing dismay, one by one as the gifts were unwrapped, the givers broke out into guffaws, and the receivers hooted at the presents—a battery-operated red button that said, 'Bullshit alert! Bullshit alert!' when you pressed it, or a child's Barbie Princess Jewellery set, or a pencil sharpener in the shape of a dog that vibrated when you put the pencil into its arse end. It was perfectly clear, from the ripple of sniggers and glances and thigh slaps and *you bastards*, whose gift was bought by whom. He opened his own present—an office voodoo doll with pins to stick into the boss—and Sandy Box roared with laughter, and he nodded and made himself smile, constructed a brief and hopeless joke about how Sandy better watch out now, and the pile of presents dwindled. Stephen looked for the door. But still Mia watched him.

'You did get me this, didn't you.'

He could only stammer, 'It wasn't supposed to be *offensive*,' before Mia shook her head in disbelief, and gathered up the wrapping paper around her cup as if, it seemed to Stephen, to get it ready for tossing into the garbage. One present had remained on the table then. Vegan Georgia, a film student with a buzz cut and a Celtic tattoo on her muscular upper arm who worked casual shifts in the kiosk (she wouldn't handle the burgers), unwrapped the gift in her lap in humourless silence. She sighed as she picked up a tiny red shiny shred of fabric with black nylon lace.

Stephen said, 'What is it?' and Georgia said without expression, 'A G-string'. At the same moment Mia began to laugh and laugh in her little high cackle. Georgia got up, wearily, shoved the G-string into the back pocket of her cargo pants, and walked out of the room.

That was last year.

Now the weight of Stephen's rummaging made the envelope dip in Mia's grasp. 'Hurry up,' she said. Then, running a disdainful glance up and down his grimy, sweat-soaked clothes, she added: 'What are those pants?'

He looked down. 'I told you, I had to clean—'

She smirked. 'They're *chef's* pants.'

Oh, he was tired of this. 'They're just pants,' he said weakly, as loyal Russell said, 'Well, he is a chef. Sort of.'

Mia snorted.

'They're not chef's pants!' said Stephen. 'They're just pants, with checks. I got them at Aldi.'

Even Russell began to smile.

'They're comfy,' Stephen muttered.

'They're chef's pants,' the others said in unison.

He held the little folded piece of paper in his fingers.

'And you were late,' said Mia. Russell looked at Stephen sympathetically and shook his head. 'Marilyn is pissed off,' Mia added cheerfully.

Stephen hated her quite completely now. '*Sorry,*' he said, trying to drip with sarcasm, 'but I had a car accident.' He found his voice faltering.

Both Mia and Russell looked at him with suspicion. 'You look all right to me,' said Mia.

'I hit someone,' Stephen said faintly. 'A pedestrian.'

Mia still looked dubious, but Russell said 'Shit, really? Are they all right?'

'I don't know.' Stephen felt lightheaded again. It was a relief to unburden himself. He heard his voice go high and husky. 'I wanted to take her to hospital but she said just drop me here so I went into the methadone clinic with her and tried to get the staff to make her see a doctor. But she wouldn't.'

'Shit,' said Russell.

'*Methadone* clinic?' Mia sneered. 'A junkie!'

Stephen nodded. 'And the nurse didn't even—'

Mia said, 'She's a *junkie*, you moron! She probably didn't even feel it. She was probably out of it.'

'She hit her *head* on the road,' Stephen said, and there it was again before him, the plummet, the flimsy birdlike body, the smack on bitumen. He thought, with horror, that he might start to cry. He turned to Russell for support, but Russell was tilting his head from side to side, as if struggling to decide something. 'Was it her fault?'

'I think so. I think she ran into the road, but I don't really—'

'Don't worry about it then, mate. She get your number plate?'

'What do you mean?' Stephen was confused. 'I left them my phone number.'

'*What!*' Both Mia and Russell stared, incredulous.

'You idiot!' said Mia. 'She'll have you in court and take you for everything you've got!'

Even Russell raised an eyebrow. 'Interesting.'

'But—you *have* to give them your phone number. She might be really hurt.'

'Not hurt enough to go to hospital,' Mia said. 'Probably not hurt enough not to steal stuff.'

'Have you checked your wallet?'

'Jesus,' he said, shaking his head at them. But had to stop his hand going to his back pocket as he mentally checked.

'My sister had a junkie boyfriend once,' Mia said. 'They're all scum, and they all lie. If she dies she deserves it. Probably would've OD'd anyway.' She swung the empty envelope between a finger and thumb, and added, 'The teambuilding thing is about to start. Marilyn is going to be late because she's got a meeting about beverages for the press conference.'

The press conference was about one of the zoo's Bengal tigers, Annabelle. It had injured itself, got an infection in the wound and died. There was to be a memorial service next week; the sponsors were invited and all the zoo staff would be allowed an hour off to attend. There was also to be an independent inquiry, and counselling was available. The word 'closure' had been used more than once.

'It's so *awful*. Poor Annabelle.' Mia's eyes moistened, large and mournful. She turned on her high heels and strode off.

The birdcall that had been reaching a crescendo suddenly stopped, and in its absence a moment of full, beautiful silence fell down upon the kiosk. The Komodo dragon, its lumpen handlike feet stretched out, lay unmoved beside its wall.

Stephen unwrapped the tiny folded piece of paper in his palm. In neat schoolgirl's writing with a love heart over the *i*, it said *Mia*.

Attendance at the Hospitality and Catering Division Facilitated Team Event was compulsory. In the past four years they had done Graffiti Skool (*creativity in a can!*), Licence to Spy, in which they pretended to be secret service agents, and Hollywood Team Building. In that they had to break into small groups and make a short film showcasing their future vision for hospitality and catering.

Stephen's approach to the clammy embarrassment of these afternoons was a furious, blind obedience—he would wear the hats, chant the catchcries, beat the drums, he would do whatever was required to get through the prolonged hours while drawing the least attention to himself. But Russell embraced these events as an opportunity for subversion. When their film was shown—a seven-minute close-up of the kiosk brick wall made while Russell had a cigarette, with a soundtrack of an elephant moaning and a forklift's reverse-gear beep—he told the audience of kitchen hands, checkout operators and cleaners from the food hall that his project was in the Dadaist tradition.

As much as Stephen admired Russell's chutzpah he grew anxious if the attention it drew lapped over onto him. While Russell strutted and the catering workers chortled, Stephen's gaze was drawn always to the back of the auditorium, where Marilyn Parris stood leaning stiffly against the wall, arms folded, unamused. Stephen and Russell had twice been called in for a counselling appointment with human resources.

Now Stephen shuffled through the open doors of the conference room. A couple of whiteboards had big cactuses drawn on them in green texta, and COYOTE CANYON printed below in red.

A perky young woman wearing a cheap red felt cowboy hat and a red chequered shirt tied in a knot at her waist greeted him. As he followed her in her tight blue jeans and cowboy boots, Stephen pictured the girl getting dressed for work this morning: painting the oversized freckles across her cheeks and nose with eyebrow pencil, twisting her blonde hair into plaits that somehow turned up at the ends. Did they have wire in them? He supposed she liked her job.

She led him across the room to where Russell sat glumly on his stackable plastic chair beside Patricia Alvarez from catering concepts, Denis Leung from functions, and Mia. They all wore red neckerchiefs at their throats except for Mia, who had tied hers around her wrist to give herself a commando-hippie air, and sat examining her fingernails.

'Howdy Pardners,' a stocky young man cried from the stage. His offsiders—the woman who led Stephen in and another one who looked the same except with brown hair—hollered back in encouraging reply.

'I'm Nestor, your pardner in crime for the next two hours, and we're the gang from Adrenaline Learning!' bellowed the man. He too wore a neckerchief and jeans, like the others, but also a real cowboy hat and a distinctive fringed leather waistcoat, as well as cowboy boots with quite high heels. Maybe he had created the game because he already had the cowboy gear.

Nestor began shouting out the rules of Coyote Canyon, which Stephen found intricate and difficult to under-stand. The game involved opponents of bandits and sheriffs and Indians, and a system of trading for vittles.

'That's the river,' said Denis Leung, pointing at a strip of butcher's paper laid over the carpet. 'If you cross anywhere but the bridge'—another paper strip—'the sheriffs are allowed to shoot you.'

The sheriffs were Meredith Kingston from promotions and a large, square-built mini-train driver, a man Russell had always claimed was Serbian. The pair stood at the edge of the river, looking at their little silver cap-guns, not speaking to each other.

'Here,' said Russell, tossing a neckerchief at Stephen. 'Put this on, or Slobodan might take you out.'

Suddenly the room filled with deafening banjo music, and Nestor waved a toy gun above his head. 'You have an hour to fill your sacks. Naw, GIT!' he screamed over the music and popped his starter gun.

People began rushing about the room, waving tickets and shouting at one another, creating crushing bottlenecks on the butcher's paper bridge across the river.

Stephen had no idea what they were supposed to do. Russell shrugged. Patricia and Denis trotted off to join the crowd. Mia eventually unwound her legs and sighed, 'Give me your tokens, you idiots.' Russell and Stephen emptied their tickets into her hands. Then she strode off across the room, ignoring the bridge, marching over the river to the merchants.

'Hey, Radovan!' Russell yelled at the mini-train guy, who glared, then followed Russell's pointing finger to see Mia. He stomped towards her with his gun out.

Stephen and Russell began to titter, watching on.

Patricia and Denis shuffled back to them, still holding their tickets and the team's A4 sheet of rules. The music jangled, people shouted. Then Russell stood up. Stephen expected him to say he was going out for a fag, but instead he said to Patricia, 'Let me have a look, see if we can figure this bullshit out.'

Stephen stared as Patricia wordlessly handed over the sheet. Russell read silently, and then looked up. 'Tell Mia to give you half the tokens, and bring the rest to me. And tell her to stay out of the fucking river.'

Patricia and Denis, astonished, did as they were bid. As they moved off Stephen smirked, waiting for the joke to happen. But Russell turned his blue eyes to Stephen and said, 'I've got another job.'

Stephen swallowed. 'What?'

Russell licked his lips, didn't look at Stephen. 'Management. Parris is leaving.'

Stephen was incredulous. 'You're joking.'

Russell exhaled a big sigh. 'You'll be right, mate. You can have this job.'

Stephen nodded, slowly. 'Shit,' he said. They both knew any job in the kiosk would be unbearable if Russell left. He nodded again, to show he forgave Russell even though he didn't.

The banjo music scrambled the air. Stephen sat on his plastic chair, trying to breathe, trying to think of coming to the kiosk without Russell, to imagine Russell sitting in an office at a computer, wearing chinos and ironed shirts. Having client meetings, talking to staff about targets and customer service.

Stephen stared at his friend. 'But why?' he whispered.

Russell shook his head and sighed at the floor. 'I dunno. Partly, Lucy wants to buy a place.' He bit his lip, then straightened and met Stephen's eyes with his. 'I'm forty-three, for Christ's sake.'

He looked over to where Mia and Patricia were sharing out the pile of paper tokens.

'I'm just sick of living like a fuckwit, mate,' Russell said. He gave a dark, horrible grin. 'I'm sick of it.'

And he got to his feet and in the din and the shouting and the banjo music he walked across the butcher's paper bridge to the other side of the river.

Stephen, alone on his plastic chair, could not believe what he had just heard. He was overtaken once more by the almighty tiredness, worse than before. He wished he could drop to the floor, fall into an unstirring sleep as deep and silent as death.

He forced himself to stand—his head was heavy on his neck, his limbs slow and thick—and walked out past the freckled girl and the whiteboards, past the blaring speakers. He walked out of the cool gloom of the conference centre into the glaring white daylight.

When he was far enough that he could no longer hear the banjo music or the shouting he stopped. He listened to the shickering of the eucalyptus leaves and the high syncopated trillings of the birds above him. He found the shade of some trees near the macaques' enclosure, sat down on a low wooden bench and rested his chin in his hands.

None of the monkeys was to be seen. They were inside sleeping, staying out of the heat—all except for the biggest male. Stephen glimpsed it now. It sat at the rear of the enclosure, squatting by a wall, considering a corn cob gripped in its fist. Stephen was reminded of something, but couldn't think what. He watched the monkey's long red face peering from beneath the shelf of its brow and wondered if it were true, that the creature was as filled with uncertainty as humans were. In computer game experiments macaques apparently skipped the tricky questions, which researchers said proved they understood when they were likely to make an error. They knew when they didn't know. The scientists were elated, but to Stephen it seemed a terrible thing, to inflict self-doubt on a monkey.

The macaque lifted its head and returned Stephen's gaze across the enclosure. Then he made the connection: it was the homeless man across the road from Stephen's house that the monkey resembled. It delivered the same stare of wounded disbelief.

This was why people didn't like medical experiments on monkeys these days. If chimpanzees shared almost all our DNA, it meant they might *understand*. Even the coldest-hearted scientist surely could not drill into the head of a creature who could stare back at him the way the macaque was staring at Stephen now. A drowned mouse's brain might not reveal everything you wanted, but at least you wouldn't have to dream about it.

Stephen closed his eyes and put his head in his hands. What did Russell mean, he was sick of how he lived? From far off, the amplified twang of surf-guitar music floated up: the seal show was beginning. When Stephen first started work at the zoo he used to take his lunch down to the performing seal show and sit in the bleachers with the punters while he ate. An open-faced young keeper wearing a bucket of fish tied to his waist would keep up a light, entertaining patter while one or other of the trained seals—Bindi or Fifi or Rocky or Miff—slid and rocked on cue beside him, waddled up some stairs to dive from a height, dipped its head and croaked when he asked it a question (sometimes the seal began the answer before the question was finished, in which case no fish), or shot into the pool on command, swimming up and down against the glass wall of the pool to demonstrate its amazing natural abilities for the audience. The crowd roared with delight as the animal carried a ball on its nose, wobbled to a Britney Spears song, swam with one flipper out of the water 'pretending' to be a shark, and delivered with various antics the conservation messages buried in the keeper's patter. Stephen wondered if the young man with the microphone sometimes longed simply to shout, 'Don't dump your rubbish in the ocean, you arseholes!' instead of what he did say, which was 'We all love to have fun at the beach, but sometimes we leave more than sandcastles behind!', while the seal emerged from the water wearing a specially tailored piece of plastic 'garbage' and pretended to be caught in its net.

Stephen sat and listened to the floating lecture and the audience applause coming through the trees. What did Russell mean, living like a fuckwit? He lived the way Stephen lived. They were a team, Russell had always said. They stood shoulder to shoulder, holding fast against the great, relentless tide of morally bankrupt, materialist mediocrity of contemporary life, lived out by cretins. That's what he had said.

Stephen's phone vibrated. In all the noise of the auditorium he had missed two more calls from Cathy. He deleted the messages. But he could no longer avoid her. She would keep calling, growing more and more irate each time he didn't answer. He dialled her number. He must simply keep calm, and get off the phone as soon as possible.

Just then Marilyn Parris appeared beside Stephen. 'What are you doing?'

He looked up at her and pressed 'end call'. Saved.

'Sorry,' he said. 'Just felt a bit off-colour.' She stared at him, waiting, while he put the phone back in his pocket. The security tag round her neck reflected a hard, square glint of light.

'I'm fine now though,' Stephen said, and followed her back into the auditorium.

The game was over. The teams huddled on their plastic chairs, untying their neckerchiefs and counting their money. The banjo music faded softly away, and Nestor stepped back up to the microphone, grinning and shaking his head in an exhilarated way.

'Folks, we hope you had as much fun in Coyote Canyon as we did,' he said. His voice took on a calm, brotherly tone. 'How many of you have played Coyote Canyon before?'

His offsiders looked around the room, as if spotting for auction bids. 'Nobody? Wow,' said Nestor. He turned to the women; they made exaggerated faces of surprise.

'Aside from all the fun, what do you think today's game has been about?' he asked the room.

Someone at the back of the room called out, weakly, 'Teamwork.'

Nestor smiled. 'Good. What else?'

A few more suggestions were tossed up: Coping with pressure. Working within the right boundaries. Nestor nodded sagely at each one, eyes closed. Stephen watched Russell in silence. And then Russell, arms folded and staring at the floor, called out in a clear, audible voice, as

Stephen knew he now must: 'Entrepreneurship.' Everyone stared. Russell did not look up from his boots at the end of his outstretched legs. He stared and stared at his boots, tapping the toe-tips against each other, slow and rhythmic.

Up on the stage Nestor opened his eyes. 'So you see,' he said, his voice low and soft now. 'You have played Coyote Canyon before. The truth is, you all play Coyote Canyon—*every, single, day*.'

The music began to rise again, and Nestor snapped back into cowboy mode. 'We've been Adrenaline Learning, and you've been *great!*' he screeched, tossing his cowboy hat in the air.

Patricia Alvarez began collecting neckerchiefs, flushed with pleasure. 'Wasn't that marvellous!' she said, beaming at Stephen and Russell. They didn't speak. As they made their way from the hall, Russell joined the small band lining up to enter their names on an attendance list on the door for the next exercise: (MANAGEMENT ONLY) GOING DEEPER, WIDER.

Stephen left the building and trailed down the stairs, drenched once more by sweat and the suffocating air. The Coyote Canyon banjo and the seal show music grew louder, merging into a single hysterical, jangling anthem.

It occurred to Stephen then that he and Russell and the others, the seals and the rhinos and monkeys, were all the same. They were all just captive animals, performing tricks for food.

CHAPTER 4

It was so quiet here.

Stephen had never liked to admit how soothed he was to walk the streets of Longley Point, how velveted by silence he was, how the moneyed suburb's gentility allowed his body to soften and forget itself. It was only in Fiona's suburb that he realised how physically alert he was to violence in his own. Even the air was cooler here. He was grateful, this of all afternoons, for the great corridors of shade created by the arching of the plane tree limbs across the streets. His socks were sweaty rags, his shoulders ached from the weight of his backpack.

In Longley Point the houses were large and hardly visible but for glimpses of glass and steel and timber, set back from the road behind freshly rendered brick fences and high, well-maintained hedges. The streets were wide and quiet. No sub-woofer hip-hop thuds emanated from cars; they glided by, black Saabs and four-wheel drives, silver Lexuses and Mercs. At the busy Vietnamese restaurant nearest Stephen's house in Norton the owners had a hairy little dog named Lexus, and at the end of the evenings when enough customers had gone they let it tear through the restaurant, leaping from chair to chair. Stephen didn't think the dogs in Longley Point were named after luxury cars. Here nobody screamed in the street to get someone's attention. Nobody wore clothes plastered with obscene images or threatening slogans. Stephen thought of the Lebanese boy on the bus. HARDEN THE FUCK UP.

As he walked he peered through the doorway of the butcher in the small strip of Longley Point shops. It was one of only two shops selling food; the rest were spacious, wooden-floored showrooms with a small white table and a tower of bangles here, a rack of six shapeless shreds of dun-coloured women's clothing there, and a black wooden plate the size of a cartwheel on the floor. In those shops nothing cost under two hundred dollars.

In the butchery, a woman with a ponytail stood with her daughter before the cabinet of meat. A sign on the window declared everything free range or organic; the shop walls were plastered with laminated magazine articles showing photographs of pigs and lambs running free in lush green pastures. The butchery customers were well informed about their dinner's quality of life before they met it; they could congratulate themselves on their concern for every moment of the animal's existence. Except for the end, Stephen thought. The hanging upside-down electrocution, or the throat-slitting or neck-wringing or bolt to the head. There were no pictures of that.

The woman was dressed in the Longley Point way— small white t-shirt, tight jeans, shiny black Birkenstocks on her slender feet. The girl wore the fresh blue uniform of one of the suburb's private schools. Stephen supposed they were mother and daughter, though the mother only looked about thirty. All the adults here looked young. It was something he had noticed often, walking the streets of Fiona's suburb. Now he wondered again how such young people could possibly have amassed so much wealth. It was at times like this he felt his country boy's naiveté most keenly. He imagined his parents wandering these streets, and knew they would be as bewildered as he was. In Rundle, money was made by farming or small business or, in the upper echelons, dentistry. It was made from things you could see and touch—teeth, wool, sports equipment, radiator parts. But in the city, it had dawned on Stephen some years ago, there were millions of invisible, indescribable jobs which produced nothing tangible, but spun inconceivable levels of wealth. Twenty years after coming to live here he still had absolutely no idea of what these jobs could look like. He felt a simpleton when people—like Fiona's friends from her marriage—said things like 'futures trader', or 'hedge fund manager', or 'chief risk officer' or 'group executive, people and strategy'. What *were* these jobs, he wanted to ask, but knew he never could.

He came to a shop selling things for pets. Kreature Kumforts, said the sign. The first few months he had passed by this shop Stephen thought it sold things for children; its window display bore the bright colours and dangling, playful lettering of a toyshop. Only one day when he stepped inside to buy some little treat for the girls did he realise the balls and climbing frames, the hairbrushes and printed t-shirts and snugly rugs were not for babies but for dogs and cats. There were doggy sweatshirts with baseball-team lettering spelling out 'woof' across the backs. There was a plastic contraption called a doggy drinking fountain that filtered and aerated continuously moving water to keep it fresh. There were, unbelievably, 'Tushie Wipes' for cats' and dogs' arses, like the ones for human babies' bums. Stephen had stood and gaped.

Now his phone began its long, insistent vibrations in his pocket. He looked at the number, closed his eyes, and swallowed.

'Hi Cathy.'

His sister launched in. Their mother had called her about next weekend, upset because Stephen had said he might be coming alone, but then Fiona had seemed fine about it, so what the fuck was going on? And why was he not answering his phone?

'Cath, just don't worry about it,' Stephen said, staring into the window of the pet shop. He could still smell on himself the musty, rancid oil. The window display had a rock-star theme: there was a doggy Elvis suit, a range of rhinestone charms and Tiffany hearts to hang from cat collars. At the back of the display hung a curtain of multicoloured leads studded, the labels said, with Swarovski Crystals.

'What do you mean, don't worry about it? Mum's invited all those people. She's desperate to see Fiona and the girls.'

Stephen said coldly, 'If Mum would just stick her nose out of it everything would be fine.'

In the window a trolley held stainless steel bowls with silver cloches propped open to reveal packets of dog chocolates and Licky Treats of liver and kangaroo. He knew what his mother would say to all this, and it would not be *poor creature*. It would be: To think, there are children starving in Africa.

Cathy paused, but she was only warming up. 'So what's going on?' she demanded.

'It's just none of anyone's business,' he said weakly. But then, rising to anger: 'The party is a stupid bloody idea anyway. And why the hell is Mum calling *Fiona*, for Christ's sake?'

Cathy sighed. Stephen knew exactly the face she would be making, standing with her raised forearm resting along some shelf, her forehead on her arm, glaring at the ground.

'Oh, you're joking,' she said.

Stephen looked at a stand of DVDs. *Kitty Goes Hunting*. *Kitty goes Fishing*. These were nature DVDs for cats.

'I don't believe it. No, actually, I do,' said Cathy.

So she knew. He had known all day, in his guts, that if he spoke to Cathy she would somehow know. Oh, he hated sisters.

'Listen—' he said firmly, desperate to shut her up, but she interrupted: 'You're going to dump her. You are. You stupid, stupid boy.'

Stephen's head began to throb. He iced his voice: '*Listen*, Cath—'

'Why do you want to live like this?'

His little sister, but how she loved to sound older than both of them, how *weary* with wisdom. 'Live like *what!*'

She was silent. Then she said, more brightly, 'Did you see that nature doco on TV last night?'

He longed to trust this change of subject. But he knew it was a trap.

'It was all about evolution.' She was furious. More than furious; she was on the verge of tears. 'And they started talking about maladaptive behaviour—you know, the sort of behaviour that's counterproductive to an individual's survival. And I thought, that's Stephen! That's my brother!'

He could not believe his ears. Cathy, whose own life consisted of working at a pharmacy and watching *Master-Chef*, lecturing him with some snatch of pseudoscience from the Discovery Channel. He snorted, but she said, 'It's true. You do it every time. Give me one good reason why you're dumping her.'

'I have reasons,' he said.

But she crowed: 'See? You don't even *know* why!'

He leant his head against the glass of the window and said with stiff dignity, 'I won't cause Fiona unnecessary pain. I'm going to—'

Cathy snorted. 'You fucking idiot,' she said. '*She'll* be fine. *You're* the one who won't be.'

He stared at the catnip teabags and the beef-flavoured beer for dogs.

'I figured out why it's so perfect that you work at the zoo, actually,' she said then. 'You like your life forms behind bars or glass, so you don't have to get in there and wrangle with any of it. You don't have to engage with it. You can just *watch*, from a distance, and whenever you get sick of it you can just walk away.'

Oh, she could fuck off.

'Whatever you say, Cath,' he said, as slow and coldly as he could. 'I have to go. Tell Mum I'll talk to her later—' His mother. Into Cathy's accusing silence he said gruffly, 'Is she alright? Her health, I mean?'

'Stephen,' said Cathy in a dead voice, 'as if you have ever given a shit about anyone but yourself.' And she hung up in his ear.

He sighed, gulped air; it was like inhaling oily bathwater. His body was heavier than he had ever known it. When, *when* would the cool change come?

Cathy was so full of bullshit. He made an indignant mental note to report this to Russell, but then Russell's words stung him again. Living like a fuckwit. What did that *mean*? He wiped a hand over his sticky head and neck. The mask of his face was now thick, mouldering rubber; he longed to peel it away. He pictured his real face beneath, melted, a grey knob of candlewax.

Each shop doorway he passed sent out a plume of luscious air-conditioned cool. He kept on walking.

Everything had grown confused and tangled. All he knew was that he needed to be free of it, of all of it. He must empty his mind of these unbearable things—Cathy, his mother, Russell, the junkie girl. Fiona. At the end of this day he would be liberated.

He must find a way to fill his mind. He turned his thoughts to the junk in the pet toy store, the DVDs and clothes and beer. A whole industry existed, livelihoods were made by the lavishing of human gifts on animals. In the paper last week he had seen a review of a café for dogs. They sat at tables, eating organic pasta and drinking juice; no human food was served. Stephen had found this incredible, but anyone he mentioned it to simply cried out, 'How cute!' That place—and the clothes and toys, the Christmas presents and special doggy cupcakes—existed because of the mysterious longings of people like Jill and Nerida.

He knew there was something about animals he could not perceive, that this was a deficiency in him. For even people who did not dress their dogs in silly clothes were able to find something serious, something profound in a creature's company. When animal people looked at a dog or a lion or a meerkat or a monkey they perceived a fellow being where Stephen only saw a bundle of muscle, a package of alien hair and foetid, frightening breath. He didn't like to look into the eyes.

Georgia from the kiosk was one of these animal people. She claimed to prefer the company of animals; they were less barbaric, more peaceable. She abhorred the word *pet.* She called her dog her 'non-human companion', she was its guardian, not owner. Her bike helmet was stickered with the slogan 'meat is murder'. She saw animals as individuals with lives of purpose and meaning, with personhood. She and Russell argued day after day about animal rights, Russell lifting dripping baskets from the fryer and Georgia stuffing chips into cartons. It mattered not, Georgia said, that animals had no concept of a future, and anyway, how could Russell possibly know this? They often had sophisticated communication systems, and organised societies of immense complexity. Many species grieved for their dead. They had not destroyed the planet with their hubris, as foolish humans had done. One day Georgia, flushed with triumph, brandished an article in which the world's greatest sperm whale expert offered evidence that the whales were capable of abstract thought and may have *formed their own religion*. Russell had snorted and said if that was her evidence for the sophistication of animals she was well and truly fucked.

(This was good. Even Cathy's outburst could be nudged off in this way, like something brought in on the tide. You just went in up to your knees dragging the unpleasant things she had said, and then shoved at them, and the waves drew them away. Maladaptive behaviour. She was so full of shit.)

How could it be, he kept puzzling as he walked, that a pet was a person? A cat wearing jewellery would still drag its arse over the carpet. A dog in an Elvis suit still ate its own vomit, would crush a mouse's warm body with its teeth, or gobble up another dog's shit. Georgia would say they were simply unencumbered by human repressions—at which Russell would snigger his old joke about why dogs licked their balls—but Stephen remained nonplussed.

It wasn't that he wanted to feel this way, about animals. But he sensed no bond, no likeness. The overwhelming, simple fact was that when he looked at Jill and Nerida's Balzac he saw no link between the dog and himself at all. When he looked into Balzac's face all he saw was otherness.

It had always been this way. His mother's stocky black bitser, Leia, was elderly, three-legged and arthritic, but even when she was young, Leia had never functioned as a playmate or the focus of human longing. Like her predecessor, Buster, she simply *was*, lying in the sun on the back verandah, or placidly lapping water from a faded plastic bowl beneath the tap. Stephen recalled only one moment as a boy when he was troubled by his family's lack of emotion toward their pets: after watching an episode of *Lassie* on television, he had sought out the mutt, Buster, where he lay in the shade beneath the station wagon. He didn't come when Stephen called him, so he hauled him out by the collar and prodded at him until he sat up, in order that Stephen could fling his arms around the dog's neck and nuzzle his face into his fur, saying *Good boy, Buster. How I love you, boy.* The dog had sat stiff, ever patient, and endured this unexpected assault, simply tilting its head the smallest degree away from Stephen's face. When he had finished and let go his collar the dog slunk back beneath the car and would not come out again.

The junkie girl came unbidden to Stephen's mind. Did she have a dog, that would sit by her as she died? But he could not allow her to come trailing back into his thoughts. He took a deep breath, and exhaled her from his mind. She must be forgotten. This seemed possible now, for she was no longer his affair, here in Longley Point. Here in the green, cushioned air she was as irrelevant as dust. Perhaps this was one of the reasons everyone here looked so clean, so young: they had no other, darker world to carry in their nerves, no public sobbing echoed in their ears. The grime and violence and anguish could not enter their bodies, because here it simply did not exist.

In his pocket the phone buzzed once, and then again. He groaned, fuck *off*. If he were in a film he could throw the phone away. He fantasised hurling it into the traffic, if there was any. He could walk away, light as a feather.

Instead he drew it from his pocket. The first message was from an unrecognisable number. RTA COURTESY SMS, it said. VEHICLE REG. SDY 768 TOWED FROM NO-STOP ZONE QUEEN ST NORTON PENALTY $198 CALL 1300 230 230 FOR VEHICLE RETRIEVAL.

Fucking hell.

But even as he read, he welcomed its cool, automated, emotionless efficiency. Why could not all communication be like this? Here is the crime, there is the penalty.

The other message was from Cathy, two words: PLEASE DON'T.

In his mind he sent the phone spinning through the air, landing *crack* on the road, exploding into a thousand tiny electronic pieces.

He turned into Fiona's street—and as he looked down its length to the cement fencepost of her house where a pair of balloons fluttered, a new, overwhelming surge of fear came flooding in. The balloons beckoned, and he understood that all the day's ordeal so far—the junkie girl, his mother, Russell's betrayal, Cathy—all of this had been nothing. It had been respite, and now it was over. The dreadful time was now. He could do nothing to stop it; it had already begun.

About a hundred metres from Fiona's front gate Stephen saw a pale pink delivery van parked at the kerb, with a thick pair of woman's legs hanging from its side door. As he drew closer he read, in purple sparkly cursive text on the passenger door, *Fantastic Fairies. Servicing the Greater Metro Area*, and a mobile phone number.

The legs, in pink lycra tights, lifted and hovered unsteadily above the guttering, and now Stephen could see a whole woman, sitting back on the floor of the van, struggling into a pair of wings. She wore a spearmint-green stretchy body suit, and a long purple tutu made of leaves of synthetic-looking transparent material. The layers of tutu fell all about her on the dirty floor of the van as she shrugged her way into the wings.

'Are you Fairy Flower?' Stephen glanced up the road to Fiona's gate and leaned into the van. He looked down at the woman's large bare feet waving above the gutter. One of them had a bunion.

'Am today,' the woman said in a monotone, and then grunted as she sat up, pinching and pulling at the tight elastic of the wings at her armpits.

She looked about forty-seven. She stared at him out of her pouchy eyes. The unlikely circlet of plastic flowers around her head, and the deep creases around her mouth, gave her a hard-knock, washerwoman's air. Andy Capp's cartoon wife came to Stephen's mind.

Now she reached behind her and hauled a plastic toolbox on to her lap. She had a stocky torso and her bust was the solid, all-of-a-shelf kind. Her calf muscles were thick and angular in the nylon leggings.

'Oh. I'm going to the party,' said Stephen.

'Right,' said the fairy, ignoring him and flipping open the toolbox. It was filled with cosmetics: trays of eye shadow, little bottles of foundation, lipsticks, fake eyelashes and bottles of sparkly stuff.

Stephen heard a child's shout float up from Fiona's backyard.

'Um, do you think you should be doing this here?'

Fairy Flower had upended a glug of foundation into one of her large palms and was busy slapping it over her face. 'What?' she said, not looking at him but peering into a small tilted mirror on the opened lid of the toolbox.

'I mean, the kids might see you. They think you're a real fairy.'

She kept slapping the foundation on and then rubbed and pushed at her face with both hands to smear it over her skin, jutting her chin. 'They won't see me,' she grunted.

Stephen looked up the street again. Three pink and purple balloons fluttered from Fiona's gatepost.

'Well, they might,' Stephen said. After a pause, he said, with more emphasis, 'They easily could. They're just there.' He gestured. The heat was even more unbearable now the sun was coming from the west; he could feel it burning his neck.

She didn't answer, but glanced up at him without interest while dabbing some other pale, flesh-coloured makeup on her face. Now her skin had a jaundiced yellow hue.

'Well, if you just let me get on with it, I'll be finished soon, and they won't,' she said to the mirror.

She dipped into the tray and pulled out some eye shadow. She leant in to the mirror and swabbed her eyelids—first one, then the other, turning her head slightly in either direction—with the gaudy purple cream. Then she pulled down the lower lid of one eye and began working at the lashes with a mascara stick in a practised, surgical movement. Still ignoring him.

She should listen to me, Stephen thought. Nobody had listened to him all day. A nugget of anger formed in his gut. He glanced back at the fluttering balloons. *I could be paying her wages.*

He heard himself say, 'I'm the father.' Not quite authoritatively. It was near enough the truth.

The fairy stared at him, one eye thickly lashed, the other naked, giving her a menacing, cycloptic air. 'Oh,' she said, in a tone one might use to a child, and went back to the mascara, but not before glancing at his trousers. 'I thought you were the cook.'

Christ almighty.

'Well I'm not. These aren't—listen. I'm the *father*.' A flush of real rage bloomed upwards in him now with the lie, and he liked it, the sound and the force of it. The weight of the word pulsed in him. 'And I'm . . . well, I'm—'

Fairy Flower stood up. 'What? *Paying my wages?*' She sneered it, and then took a step towards him, eyeing him steadily, her face garish and alarming in the doll's makeup. She was almost Stephen's height. She rolled her shoulders, jerking them back and forth, and then reached behind herself with one hand to yank on one of her wings.

'Listen, you dickhead. This is my daughter's gig, only she's got gastro suddenly. I'm a fucking para*medic*—' she gave her substantial bust a single, vigorous thrust, which appeared to settle the wing discomfort—'and I've just come off an eleven-hour shift saving the lives of bigger arseholes than you, but to save my daughter's gig I've come here to entertain your little girl and her friends. So I don't need any shit from you. Understand?'

She stood there in front of the open door of the van, hands on her heavy hips, the tips of her nylon gossamer wings only just peeking out from behind her shoulders.

'Oh,' said Stephen. He could imagine her wrestling drunks to the ground, plunging needles into flesh. 'Okay. Sorry.' He nodded.

The paramedic fairy put one foot into the van and heaved a shiny pink velour blanket towards her. Into the middle of the blanket she dumped a purple plastic tub filled with little coloured plastic bags, bulging with lollies and cheap plastic trinkets. Then she gathered up the blanket to make a sack, the bucket inside it, and swung it over her shoulder.

'Hold this,' she ordered, shoving a crimson plastic wand into Stephen's hand, and turned to drag the van door shut.

'Now, I have to make some calls, and get something to eat. Tell—' she looked through the window at a piece of paper on the passenger seat '—Fiona, that I'll be there in half an hour.'

'Okay,' said Stephen. 'I'm, um, sorry about . . .'

But Fairy Flower simply held out her hand for the wand. Stephen handed it to her, and turned and tried not to run the rest of the way to Fiona's house.

He crossed the shallow lawn and stepped on to Fiona's wide, cool, tiled verandah. He swallowed, peering into the gloom of the house. He must prepare himself. Get through the party, then do it, then leave. And then this dreadful day, the longest of his life, would end.

'Oh, you're *here*.'

In silhouette he saw her sweeping down the hallway to fling the screen door wide, opening her house, herself, to him.

He had spent all day thinking of her but now he was here he was shocked by the physical, moving fact of her.

The humidity was confusing him, slowing his perception: she seemed to move towards him in slow motion. He saw her outstretched arms, the blue and white curlicue print of the soft Indian cotton shirt against the brown of her skin, the neckline fallen open, the string-ties dangling loose, the soft shadow of her breasts beneath. He watched her easy, unwavering stride towards him, her bare brown feet and smoothly sturdy thighs in the cut-off denim shorts. And finally he made himself meet her gaze, her calm grey eyes, that wise, sceptical smile.

She looked so cool.

He let himself be reeled in, wrapped in Fiona's arms. 'You're *burning*, you poor thing,' she murmured. She blew a long, cooling breath of air down the back of his neck and he almost sank to his knees with the sweetness of it. She kept murmuring, was he all right? She had worried about him all day. Was the girl all right? Was work unbearable?

If he could only stay like this, nuzzled into Fiona's cool neck, all his life. He descended into the layers of her smell, breathed in the light brackishness of her morning swim beneath the soapy warmth, but most of all the dank sweetness of her sweat. He rested his forehead in the curve of her neck. He wanted to lap at her skin with his tongue; to take heavy, nodding strokes at her, like a horse at a salt-lick.

She stepped back, her hands resting lightly on his shoulders, and looked into his eyes. 'What a terrible day you've had.'

Stephen saw that he could fail now, in this moment. PLEASE DON'T. He looked into Fiona's face, perhaps more closely now than any time since they had met. A strand of blonde hair fell across her high, honest forehead, which glistened faintly with perspiration. He saw her pale eyebrows that she plucked too finely, her serene, intelligent eyes bestowing her good faith upon him. He could forget it all, right now. Let go and allow himself to fall once more into the cool, deep pool of Fiona's life, and drown.

He gulped for air.

'I'm fine,' he said, and peeled her hands from his body. And then the girls came pounding down the hallway, shouting. They stood in their fairy clothes, hands on their hips. 'Did you bring me a present?' demanded Ella, blazing with entitlement, looking down at Stephen's backpack on the ground.

'Ella!' Fiona said. 'Go and brush your hair. You too, Larry. Leave Stephen alone, he needs to have a rest.'

She turned to him. 'Why don't you have a shower, cool down?' He obviously reeked.

Larry sniffed: 'It is her *birthday*.' As she turned to follow Ella's sulky retreat she peered down at Stephen's backpack, where the Kmart plastic bag protruded. She leaned towards him, asked slyly, 'Watcha get her?'

Fiona said, 'Stop it. It's rude. Go.'

Stephen shoved the forgotten My Little Pony deeper inside his backpack as they walked into the house. He would get rid of it later. He whispered to Fiona, 'I got tickets to the circus.'

Three tickets to the circus.

Fiona grinned and set a tall glass of icy water on the table for him before turning away to scrabble in her handbag on the bench. 'I think she's scared of the circus. She'll love it though. Listen, I have to run to the shops, I forgot the bloody candles. Chris and the shrew will be here soon. I'll just be five minutes? You should have a shower.'

Stephen nodded, drinking deep, and waved her away. He held the icy glass to his temple.

The Arrogant Shrew was a species of endangered mouse on the zoo's fundraising list. As soon as she read the name Fiona had started using it to refer to her sister-in-law, Chris's wife, Belinda. Stephen recalled the day Fiona came to meet him at the zoo, reading creature names aloud from the billboard list—Allen's Cotton Rat, the African Giant Free-Tailed Bat, the Bridled Nail-tailed Wallaby, the Arrogant Shrew—as they tossed coins into the spiralling donation funnel. There were hardly any coins in the Perspex tank at the bottom of the funnel. Saving animals from extinction was of little interest to zoo visitors, he had pointed out to her, unlike the gift shops and the food court, crammed with punters buying plush synthetic monkeys made in China or eating chips fried in palm oil which they ate while staring into the eyes of the orang-utan whose native habitat had been destroyed for the expansion of palm oil plantations.

Fiona had rolled her eyes as Stephen lectured, and squeezed his upper arm. 'You're a cheerful bugger, aren't you?' And she kissed him and slid her arm through his, and he was silenced by the simple pleasure of it— wandering along together, holding hands.

The next time she came she brought the girls, who soon grew bored with the real animals, finding greater joy in flinging themselves over the sun-warmed bronze statue of a giant tortoise and lounging there, or spreading their arms to measure themselves against the plastic model wingspan of the Andean condor while the real bird sulked, hunched and monstrous, on a broken branch beneath the high swags of its netted cage. At the finch cages the girls and Stephen snuck away to feed extra chips to the dirty, long-beaked white ibis which swung down from the trees and stalked throughout the zoo grounds, while Fiona stood nodding and smiling with the finch-keeper, who held her captive with the dreary details of his tiny, invisible birds.

It was only a year ago, but it felt like ten.

Stephen got out his wallet and yelled for the girls. They appeared instantly, grinning, breathless in their fairy clothes.

His girls.

Ella wore a pale mauve ribbed singlet with a Barbie logo printed across the chest in a shiny plastic transfer, and a skirt made of flimsy tongues of torn pink and purple gauze. A silver plastic tiara with one broken point sat low on her hairline, and a tight bracelet of purple plastic baubles bit into one plump wrist. She settled herself on a kitchen chair, the strips of her fairy skirt settling around her, like the puff and shiver of flamingo feathers. She grinned up at him, open-mouthed, her gappy little teeth and lips wet with spit and anticipation. Her legs and bare feet stuck out before her and she sat straight, arms at her sides, as if making a space large enough for an impossibly enormous gift to be lowered into her lap. Larry stood beside her sister, arms wound across each other, alert and watchful as a bodyguard. Her faded ballet tutu—too small for her now—was pushed below the round pot of her belly, so it stuck up at the back like pink hen feathers, the pants elastic cutting into the soft flesh of her legs.

'Okay, Ella, I have something special for your birthday.'

The girls stared, biting their lips, suddenly frightened and serious, as they were whenever extreme pleasure was imminent. Their eyes darted to Stephen's bag on the floor, then back to his hands as he pulled his wallet from his pocket, and took out the yellow paper tickets.

He leaned down. 'We're going . . . to . . . the *circus!*' he cried, flourishing the tickets.

Ella glanced at Larry and then back at him, waiting for meaning. 'Happy birthday!' he cried, leaning in to kiss her cheek. But she remained motionless, wan with polite incomprehension. Larry simply looked down at the tickets with open disgust.

Stephen said, 'These are just the tickets. But the circus will be such fun!'

His voice was strained, stupid. He pressed on. 'There will be lions, and monkeys, and camels!' He pushed the tickets into Ella's hands. 'And acrobats! You know those ladies in sparkly costumes? Hanging on trapezes?' He drew in the air, hapless. 'We'll go together—the three of us.'

Ella held the tickets, peered at them. 'What about Mum?' she asked suspiciously. The paper scraps forlorn in her hand.

'Well,' Stephen licked his lips, 'Well, maybe we will just go specially, just a special treat for the three of us.'

The girls heard his voice, thick and odd. Ella stared at Larry. Her little sister took charge, turning on him. 'But what else?' she demanded. 'Is there anything else?' She peered down at his bag. She knew there was something there, something better.

The insult went deep. 'No,' he snapped at her.

He turned back to Ella. He would appeal to her mercy, her higher self. He angled himself between her and her sister, ducked to meet Ella's gaze.

'I thought you would like this present,' he said softly. 'I thought about it really hard. I think you'll really love it. We'll have fun, and popcorn, and there will be acrobats and animals. And we will be together.'

Ella stared at him sadly. She knew her duty. She climbed down from the chair, stepped stiffly to him and kissed him coldly on the cheek. 'Thank you,' she said. In a sweet, horrible, artificial voice, she added, 'I'll put them up here so Mum can look after them,' and slipped the tickets on to the kitchen bench. Then she looked at Larry in a way that meant they had business to discuss, and walked away, her fairy skirt hanging.

But Larry was not finished with Stephen. She stood, hands on her hips. 'She's got lots of presents coming,' she declared. 'She's already got twenty dollars from Grandma and eighteen more dollars, because more from pocket money. And a *Bratz*.'

This last was meant as the knife-plunge Stephen felt it to be. Larry's hard little eyes met his in a baleful stare, and then she left.

He walked out through the French doors and across the terrace. He leaned over his crossed arms on the railing, staring out across the harbour past the sparkling white stalactites of sailboats and runabouts and fishing craft and ferries, past the bridal trails of churning water, out to the distant blue bank of the horizon where a ship rested on the quiet steady line between sea and sky. He could be out there, on that ship.

The girls would come around. He had seen this before, at parties and Christmas—children tossing aside the carefully chosen gifts (books, hand-made dolls) for any bit of plastic crap with a logo or a battery. But soon, when the plastic cracked underfoot or the batteries died, they returned to the discarded things and saw their true, instrinsic worth, and grew to love them. The girls would remember the circus; remember him.

He stared out at the ship, suddenly unsure. Maybe they would not like the circus at all. He saw them sitting in the dust and the dark, unsmiling, arms folded, as the bears danced, mangy and lumpen, in the distance. Or worse, thanking him quietly with that terrible politeness, holding in their minds the promised reward for good behaviour at home, once it was over. They might despise him for it.

The ship lay, a grey slug, on the horizon.

He had not travelled enough; hardly at all. This came to him with sudden urgency. A trip to Thailand eight years ago. Before that, Europe (which turned out to be Earl's Court and Nice) with his friend David when he was twenty-two, sleeping on someone's floor with not enough blankets, and then the dirty French youth hostel. He drank till he vomited, then lay on a spinning bed in the dark, wracked by turns with homesickness and longing for a girl passed out in the opposite bunk.

Fiona was back; he heard her opening and closing drawers in the kitchen at the same time as he heard a car door slam in the street, then Belinda's voice, and Chris's.

'They're here,' he called over his shoulder to Fiona. He heard her set a knife down on the chopping board before going to answer the door.

He had never before known the cadences of a person's movements like this, except in his own family, as a child. It was not just her tread; footsteps were easy, especially here in Fiona's house when there were just the two of them and the girls, whose hard little heels struck the floorboards like mallets. But even elsewhere, in other houses, in shops, he could tell Fiona's presence by the sound and rhythm of her movements: keys in a handbag, the taking of a breath. Surely humans could only breathe in so many ways—inhalation, exhalation could not possibly be so individual—but still, he always knew her. He knew the sound of her swallow, her bite of an apple from another room.

Belinda came clopping up the front steps, chiding Chris in her modulated customer-service voice. Belinda began most sentences with Chris's name, followed by a question that was really an instruction. Stephen sighed into his folded arms. Soon they would all be here, the whole grotesque parade of Fiona's family. Her father Pat, in his ironed jeans and tucked-in shirt, croaking about some new violation of his rights. Last time it had been Aborigines and Sorry Day ('Howbout *Thankyou* Day instead! I'd like to know where Evonne Goolagong would be without the white man!'). And nervy, bug-eyed Jeanette with her stiff hair and tidy clothes, who couldn't stop talking, never meeting your eyes but fixing her gaze instead on the rings she wore, her spotty hands forever held out before her with the fingers splayed, palms down, then up, then down again, examining then twisting and adjusting all the gold rings she never took off.

A jet ski rider began to shred the silence in the bay below the house, lifting and hurling the machine so it hit the water in violent thuds. Obnoxious fuck. Which made Stephen remember that Richard was coming too.

He dropped his head into his arms and let out a long, high, muffled cry into his own chest.

Richard. Objectionable ex-husband, wine-collecting, six-foot-four, human-fucking-rights *barrister* Richard. Expert shaver, wearer of custom-made suits and spotless, expensive sportswear. Stephen looked down at the harbour. He could throw himself down there to the Moreton Bay figs and the jutting rocks, right now. He could bawl like the mummy's boy Richard had always known he was.

Stephen hated so many things about Richard. The way he took possession of Fiona's house, as if he had never left. The things Fiona still had in the house from him, from her marriage. Books with Richard's flourished handwriting scrawled on the inside pages, or on the backs of paintings. *Darling. All my love.* Stephen had always known he could not ask Fiona to throw them out—she would be incredulous: *I use that cookbook all the time!*—but he was disturbed by this evidence of how things once were, of how Richard once knew every inch of Fiona the way that Stephen knew her now. His own fingers hooked through Fiona's belt-loop in a crowd, or her elbow crooked through his, their legs brushing one another's lazily, convivially, in bed—all of this seemed unique to him, exceptional. The idea that Fiona had done these things with someone else, someone as loathsome as *Richard*, was unthinkable.

The few times the two men had met, Richard seemed to see straight through Stephen, with his smug, appraising, rich-boy's smile and his sharp lawyer's gaze. He took one look, it seemed, and knew everything about him—his failings with money and women and jobs. Stephen knew this was fanciful, but Richard dropped little grenades into conversation, like the time he idly mentioned some exploited woman in a wage case. Could you believe how pathetically low some poor bastards' incomes were, he said—giving Stephen that level, awful stare—'like *fourteen-dollars-eighty an hour*.'

He couldn't say anything to Fiona; to suggest Richard had bothered to find out how much Stephen was paid would sound delusional. He was just a bully-boy, Stephen knew—but knowing didn't help. Anytime Richard came near him Stephen would begin to perspire, would feel himself slouch; the lawyer's presence seemed to cause his very skull to thicken, his thoughts to come sludgy and stupid. But it was worse than that. It was not that Richard caused these things; he simply revealed the deficiencies that had always been there.

A few weeks ago, when Richard arrived at the front door to collect the girls, Stephen was inside watching the cricket and he heard the bastard say coolly to Fiona, 'Still slumming it with dishwashers, are we, Fi?'

It was not Richard's barb that made Stephen flinch. It was that Fiona had tried to say something cutting in reply, but her voice had faltered; she was unnerved. Listening from the living room, Stephen felt his stomach drop.

Was she recognising some truth in Richard's words? Was this—slumming it—a realisation she had been coming to herself?

He shrank into his chair, trying to concentrate on the game. But he had heard it. Watching the players run and scramble on the screen, he began to think that maybe there was something about Fiona's embrace of him that had only ever been . . . symbolic. That perhaps his invitation into her house, her bed, was wreathed in (prompted by, even?) her ill-will towards Richard. That it was not to do with him, Stephen, at all.

Things forgotten came to him then, though he tried to stop them, sitting there that afternoon waiting for Richard to leave. He remembered dinner parties with couples in the early months, when Fiona sat with her hand on his arm, her eyes shining a little brightly as she inserted her own merry answers to whoever had asked him a question. Announcing his job before he was asked about it. 'Stephen works in a café, at the zoo. No career bullshit, no corporate wife crap. I can't tell you how refreshing.' The wives would break off from talk of their holiday houses and children to glance at him afresh, as if Fiona's words might actually convince. The men sighed, pretending envy. One of them actually said he wished he could piss off his futures job and work at something with his hands, as Stephen did.

Stephen had thought: you're doing it right now, you cock, but in reply he simply smiled and said, 'So why don't you?' After the tiniest pause the talk turned back to renovations and schools. After a few of those times the dinner parties stopped, and they took to Friday nights at home with the girls and takeaway Thai, and Stephen, he now realised, had not even noticed or cared.

Then, sitting before the television that day, Stephen heard their voices rising. Fiona's had a pleading note—'but we agreed on this!'—but Richard's came down coldly over hers. The pickup day would have to change, he was saying. Something to do with his work.

'But that's my clinic day. I'd never be able to get home in time!' Fiona begged. By the time Stephen registered the distress in her voice he found himself at the door, stepping to her side, facing up to Richard just in time to hear him say, 'You'll just have to sort something out.' Icy, a command.

'Don't think so, mate,' Stephen heard himself say. Fiona and Richard both turned to him in astonishment. Fiona's hand went to his back, took hold of his shirt. His gut rizzled and he could feel a tremor in his legs. He could not believe he was saying lightly into Richard's face, 'Sounds like you're the one who needs to sort something else out.'

And though he had to lick his lips for fear as he smiled, he felt Fiona straighten beside him, felt her grip on him relax. Then the girls came running down the hallway, and Richard—miraculously—stepped back, fondling his car keys in his huge fist, looking at Stephen with cold contempt. 'Whatever,' he said, feigning disinterest. But it was clear he was furious.

After they waved the girls off and stepped back inside, Fiona pulled herself to him, her head on his chest. 'Thank you,' she said. His legs still felt weak. He kissed her back, but waved away her gratitude as he fell back into the chair and took up the remote control. She stood behind him, put her cool hand on his neck. Then she said, 'This is why I love you,' as she left the room.

He knew she meant it. In that moment, she meant it.

But since that day it had become clear to Stephen how much he did not belong here, in her life, in this watery suburb of lawyers and Mercedes. Fiona surrounded herself with people who despised him—her parents, Richard who would now be biding his time, even her brother Chris wished him gone. Stephen knew her whole family talked about him. He did not belong in any part of Fiona's life and in the truest part of her—even if she had not yet gotten around to accepting it—she knew.

Now, as if she had heard his thoughts, she called to him from inside the house that Chris and Belinda had arrived. He could hear in her voice the playful *don't-leave-me-in-here-with-them* and *you-gotta-hear-this*—Belinda was probably going on with some entertaining new bit of shamanic nonsense. But Stephen did not want to go in there today. He wished he'd showered. He was afraid.

The jet ski rider thrust and ground his way back across the harbour.

'Stephen?' Fiona called.

Over by the fishpond something moved and then was gone. He stopped and watched, and then he saw it: the water dragon again, on the rocks of the pond. This lizard, with its curved stance, raised up on its front legs with its cement-coloured nose in the air, delighted Fiona and the girls. It had become a sort of pet—they fed it grapes, and recently a smaller one had begun to appear as well. Stephen had come across it sometimes, a piece of grey bark on the terrace that suddenly sprang alive, bolting in its waggling gait across the paving then darting out its

tongue at a fleck of something on the ground. The girls
loved the little reptiles—Ella had named one of them
Sophie—but the dragons privately alarmed Stephen: the
camouflage, their sudden presence when you had glanced
at that spot just an instant before and seen nothing.
Sometimes out here on the terrace the larger dragon
appeared and began stalking Stephen, twisting itself
towards him. He would stamp his foot on the paving,
but the dragon never moved away: just stopped, a statue
again, staring at Stephen sideways. Waiting him out. And
Stephen always found a reason to step quickly across the
pavers and draw the sliding glass door shut behind him.
You prefer your life forms behind glass. He stopped, faltered. He
shunted the door roughly closed and turned away, leaving
the dragon stock still, its back straight and narrow, head
tilted, listening for danger.

Fiona was leaning back against the kitchen bench, one
bare foot resting on the other, listening to Belinda,
biting a corner of her lip the way she always did when
amused. Stephen could tell she was gearing up for one
of her mischievous challenges.

'So I advised her, with her blood type,' Belinda was saying, 'to start with the Cleansing Series Three.' She swept about the room in a long tiered skirt and layers of opaque clothing, pulling things from her oversized leather bag and distributing them on the table and the countertop, speaking all the while in her low, confiding voice.

'Hi, Belinda,' said Stephen. As she turned Fiona grinned behind her, drawing hippy-dippy circles in the air.

Belinda was a pharmacist-turned-naturopath-entrepreneur, who owned a small but rapidly expanding chain of salons, Belinda Burton's Naturaceuticals Therapeutic Day Spas. She was also married to Mandy's ex-husband, a fact Stephen still found strange.

When Stephen's sister and Chris finally split, it was Chris everybody felt sorry for. He was the sensitive architect husband, who coped with Mandy's absences, with her curtness and anger and her strange war-reporter's life, without complaint. He had always met her decisions—including the one not to have children—with quiet, grieving acceptance. When the news of the breakup came the couple's friends immediately took Chris's side. If anyone should leave the marriage, it should have been him. Mandy's mother was among the devastated; she loved Chris, he seemed to love her. They were family. It wasn't only Stephen who suspected Chris was the son Margaret always really wanted.

But Chris and Mandy's graceful Harper Hill house would not stay empty for long. Available men of Chris's age and *calibre*, Stephen was told by more than one of his sisters' friends, were rare as hen's teeth. And then one evening Chris brought Belinda to a party where Stephen and Cathy were. He stood grasping her hand and gazing at her the whole night—an adoration she absorbed without surprise, for she was used to it. At the end of the party Chris, flush with drink and a new determination his former in-laws did not recognise, told Stephen and Cathy he was getting remarried.

Cathy went to the wedding. Stephen was invited but he made an excuse not to go. He knew Chris didn't really want him there; they had never been friends, as Chris and Cathy were. Stephen liked to think he also declined out of loyalty to his mother, who was still devastated and pointlessly hopeful that Mandy might see the error of her ways and beg Chris to allow her back.

Cathy reported that the wedding, for two atheists in their forties, was bizarre. It was in a Catholic church, because Belinda wanted sandstone in the photographs.

She wore a skin-tight, floor-length white satin dress with a train. They had flower girls, for God's sake. Not Fiona's girls but a friend's daughters; pretty, long-haired ballet types. The reception had been at a yacht club and involved a string quartet.

Cathy told Stephen this over lunch at the zoo kiosk one day. She told him too, how now that Chris and Mandy's old friends had got to know Belinda they'd gone back to Mandy's side. They'd muttered it to Cathy at the reception: what could a nice guy like Chris possibly see in Belinda?

But the siblings were unsurprised, as they sat together chewing stale foccacia. 'If I'd been married to Mandy I'd want someone easier too,' Cathy said, and Stephen nodded. He too could see the appeal—Chris no longer had a woman demanding he join her exhausting, endless challenge to the world. He could simply let go, live in a nice house, buy stuff and do what he was told. And with any luck she would be giving him a baby.

They sat at the metal table beneath the umbrella, recalling Chris's first wedding, to their sister all those years ago. The reception in the Rundle Corroboree Room, when Mandy had worn a second-hand hippie frock and the wine came from cardboard casks and the music from a portable CD player. But that was a long time ago, and the world had changed many times since then. Stephen had expected never to see Chris again.

Today Belinda wore multicoloured gemstone beads and bangles at her neck and wrists, her honey-blonde hair pulled back from her face into a chignon, held there with big fake flowers. (Stephen had once heard Cathy and Fiona deriding Belinda's clothes. They had a near-empty bottle of cheap champagne on the coffee table between them, and their conversation had a reckless air. 'It's sort of *boho,*' Fiona said when he asked, as if this was an explanation, 'which doesn't really suit her.' When he'd asked why not, Cathy said drily, 'Because she's more ho than bo,' and Fiona snorted into her glass.)

Belinda had the gaunt, hunted look of magazine women. Her skin was evenly tanned—fake, Fiona said— and her long ponytail swung and shone. She had a small nose and a bony face on a long neck. She held her spine very straight. She did a lot of Pilates. She even took the one-year-old, Aleksander, to some kind of baby yoga class, where they played special music and pulled the babies' legs around.

Now Belinda glanced at him with her customary distaste. 'Hello, Stephen,' she said, and turned back to Fiona.

Each one of Belinda's all-white shopfronts—counters, halogen-lit walls and shelving, all done out in glossy white plastic, though she called it *resin*—featured a massive backlit photograph of Belinda's face on one entire wall, with the printed Belinda Burton Naturaceuticals Pledge For Your Wellness and her flamboyant signature beneath. The Naturaceuticals product range—skin cleansers with vitamins in them, as far as Stephen could tell—was packaged in silver-and-white tubes and boxes, each banded with a small horizontal label in clean, pale green, printed with tiny black medical-looking text, giving the stuff a scientific yet ecological sort of feel.

Fiona's bathroom was full of Naturaceuticals samples given her by Belinda: shampoo, face cleanser, pore opener, eye hydrator. Fiona said all the claims were rubbish, but it smelt nice. She explained to Stephen that the shops, or *clinics*—Belinda hated it if you called them shops—provided various beauty-cum-health services: facials, 'body wraps', waxing (Stephen flinched), as well as liver analysis, iridology and something called biorhythm interpretation. Behind the counter of every shop was a hyper-lit, locked glass case containing the Naturaceuticals Wellness Supplements and Detoxification Series. The women who worked in the centres were as narrow-faced and ponytailed and glossy-haired as Belinda. Fiona said they must have to undergo hair analysis before they got the job.

Belinda grew up in a caravan park in Easton, but moved to the wealthier suburbs as soon as she could make her escape. She studied pharmacy while working two jobs, but then abandoned it for natural therapy studies. She propelled herself out of the poverty she felt doomed to by sheer force of intellect and will. Chris told all this one night to Stephen after he began seeing Fiona, when the two men attempted to alleviate the awkwardness of their knotted relationship by going to the pub together and getting rat-arsed. It didn't work.

Stephen learned that Belinda was the only child of an alcoholic taxi driver and a downtrodden nursing home aide. The pair, now elderly, had retired to a broken-down farm with a yard full of rusting vehicles beyond the mountains outside the city. Despite their regular attempts to contact her, Belinda would have nothing to do with her parents: they were *toxic*, she told Stephen much later. Riddled with dysfunction. He'd murmured in sympathy, and Belinda had eyed him and added in a cool voice, 'Most people can't recognise their own toxicity, of course.'

Toxicity and its banishment was like religion to Belinda. And it was her twaddle about toxins and metabolic wastes and chemical imbalances that most incensed Fiona. She left the energy healing and shamanism alone, but Fiona had excelled at chemistry and biology at school and was personally offended by linguistic abuses of her beloved facts. She had wanted to be a doctor until her father talked her out of it (she wouldn't be able to cope, he said, and tried to push her into nursing instead). She was still angry all these years later—as much with herself as her father, Stephen thought—at how she had capitulated into physiotherapy. Sometimes he wondered if it was the fact that Belinda had thrown away the chance to study pharmacy that fuelled Fiona's attacks on her mumbo-jumbo. And—very occasionally—he even felt a little sorry for odious Belinda, caught in the cold glare of Fiona's logic. Because Belinda would make no concession, even as Fiona demolished the ground she stood on with her direct, steady questions. Belinda's whole life depended on her faith in herbal hocus-pocus, and although Fiona was the only person who could rattle her, the faith remained unshaken.

Fiona knew she could be cruel, that Belinda was an easy target. ('She said, "Of course the pelvis is the brain of the body," and I said, "Um, Belinda, I think you'll find the *brain* is the brain of the body."') And although she still occasionally rose to the bait, after the first few forays she mostly left her sister-in-law alone.

But watching her now across the kitchen, Stephen knew this was not one of those days.

'So how does that work again, this detox thing?' Fiona asked mildly, turning to butter a stack of white bread triangles and press them into a bowl of hundreds-and-thousands.

Belinda eyed her. 'It releases the toxins,' she said, after a pause. 'By flushing them through the lymphatic system.'

'Right,' said Fiona. 'Just before we get to the lymphatic system, what are the toxins, specifically?'

'Oh,' Belinda said, 'just the accumulated waste materials which interfere with healing and metabolism.' Patiently, as though this was something everybody knew.

'But which waste materials? What are they, exactly?' Fiona was smiling lightly, looking directly at Belinda now. Stephen wished she wouldn't. He could not be entertained by this today.

Belinda pressed her glossed lips together. She paused again, but she would not back down. 'Well, as I said, the *lymphatic* system—' she began, but she was saved. The front doorbell rang, and Ella's and Larry's shouts echoed through the house. The two women made resolute smiles at each other as Fiona wiped her hands on a tea towel, rolling her eyes at Stephen as she passed him.

Belinda sighed—with relief, Stephen imagined—and began to unpack a cooler bag of organic dips and packets of organic rice crackers and organic tamari almonds on the bench. Stephen was suddenly starving. He had eaten nothing all day but the Icy Pole at work, and now a ravenous greed overcame him. He scrabbled in a plastic bowl that Fiona had set out for the kids, shoving a handful of bright yellow corn chips into his mouth. He felt Belinda's cold gaze on him as he chewed. She rezipped her cooler bag, folded it neatly away, snipped open the rice cracker packet with a pair of kitchen scissors and arranged them carefully on a plate, her movements deliberate, delicate.

'So, Belinda,' Stephen said, pretending not to notice her contempt (why was it that so many women seemed so openly to despise him?). As he spoke he found he had not quite finished his mouthful, and a fine spray of yellow corn chip escaped from his lips. 'Sorry,' he said, wiping his mouth. Belinda backed away from him with the pained face she often wore, which was possibly an attempt to smile. It was more of a wince.

Where was Chris? Stephen craned to look down the hallway. The girls and some other children clamoured out in the front yard. Then he remembered the fairy would be arriving, and he moved out of sight. He wondered if it was too early to go to the fridge and take out a beer. He had left a six-pack of Heineken here last time, he was certain. He hoped he had. He thirsted for it, wished to lick the cold green glass.

Chris arrived in the kitchen, thin and harried, pushing the enormous black stroller that Fiona privately referred to as the Hummer. Deep in the gloom of its cave lay fat, happy Aleksander.

The two men clenched awkward hands. Stephen was about to offer Chris a beer, but remembered Chris had given up alcohol. He was vegan now, too, like Belinda. Not to protect the rights of animals, like Georgia at the kiosk, but because Belinda declared that meat made you dwell in the past. She never drank alcohol, either. If she were ever offered a glass of wine she would smile and say, 'No, thank you, I prefer not to poison my body.' Belinda talked often about self-respect, and watched what other people ate and drank with open revulsion. She was also prone to placing her palm flat across her chest and emphasising that she was a mother. She included this fact in almost everything she said. These days Fiona and Stephen had to look at the floor when Belinda said things like *As a mother, I'm concerned about the environment*, because it had become one of their favourite mean jokes. 'As a mother, I need another drink,' Fiona would say. Or Stephen, lunging for the remote control: 'As a mother, I need to watch the football.' 'As a mother, I don't give a fuck about anyone but myself,' they crowed.

'I'll just go get the other bag,' said Chris. They travelled with many bags.

Stephen's desire for beer surged towards urgent. He turned back to Belinda. 'So there's a couple of empty shops in the Plaza near my place in Norton,' he said.

'Really,' Belinda said, turning into the pram's cave to unbuckle Aleksander.

'Yeah,' he said, reaching for another fistful of chips. 'Where the discount shoe shop used to be, just near the Eye of Horus.' He liked saying *Eye of Horus*. The Eye of Horus was a tiny dark shop jammed full of Egyptian trinkets and smoky with incense, not far from the fish shop. 'I thought you might be interested in it for another Belinda Burton's Naturaceuticals.'

Belinda flinched, but did not look up, grimacing as Aleksander wriggled in his seat, kicking her hand away, making it impossible for her to unbuckle the belt. 'Stop it, Aleksander,' she murmured. The baby began bucking harder.

'I could ask for you, if you want,' Stephen said.

Aleksander kicked more viciously at Belinda. She took a deep breath and tried to appear serene. She frequently explained to people that she was a very spiritual person; she had installed many stone Ganeshas in Chris's house, she burned essential oils in her spas. She sometimes wore red threads around her wrist that Stephen assumed were associated with her spiritual journey. She often left Chris with the baby for weekends while she attended expensive meditation retreats at out-of-town therapeutic spas. This had the dual advantages of tax deductibility and allowing her to spy on the opposition. Her spiritual path appeared to be separate from her business path, however—the latter was all steel efficiency. She once told Fiona about firing a distracted employee whose husband had just started chemotherapy. Belinda had no room for passengers in this life. That was another thing she often said. As a mother.

Stephen was surprised to find himself thinking 'poor Belinda' now, as he watched her at the mercy of her baby. She closed her eyes and inhaled deeply. Then she plunged her hand in once again to jab at the buckle between Aleksander's kicks. 'Stop it now, darling,' she crooned. 'You don't want to hurt Mummy, do you?'

His face seemed to indicate this was exactly what he wanted to do, but Aleksander stopped. Belinda exhaled a long, satisfied sigh, said 'Thank you, darling,' and leaned in again to the buckle. Just as she unsnapped it, Aleksander convulsed with his full body so that his hard little leather shoe connected with his mother's left eye and cheekbone in a direct, savage kick. Belinda reeled back, letting out a howl of anguish, and fell against the fridge.

'Shit,' said Stephen, and made as if to move. The wailing noise Belinda was making would not be out of place in one of Mandy's documentary reports from Gaza. At the sound of her shrieking Chris appeared, bolting into the kitchen. Belinda crouched by the fridge, two hands pressed over her eye and cheek, squatting in her swirling clothes and her expensive-looking pearl-coloured sandals. It was quite impressive, Stephen thought, how she kept her balance in those heels.

Chris took one look at the scene, taking in Stephen peering down, Belinda crouched gasping and sobbing, and cried, 'What the heck is going on!' He dropped to the floor, his arms around his wife, and stared at Stephen.

'He *kicked* me!' Belinda howled.

'What!' Chris leapt to his feet, advancing on Stephen in horror.

Stephen ran his tongue over his teeth to dislodge the corn-chip sludge. 'Not me, mate. Him.' He gestured at the pram.

Aleksander was now stretched calmly back with a bottle of water stuck in his mouth, flicking repeatedly at the bottle's nipple with his teeth in a satisfied way. His little feet pedalled the air.

Belinda unfurled from the floor, taking deep breaths and leaning on the bench. 'Chris, could you please get me a camomile tea and some arnica,' she said in a low, urgent voice, the kind of tone surgeons perhaps used to speak to one another in operating theatres.

Chris disappeared down the hallway. Belinda moved to the table, dabbing at her cheek with two fingers, then checking them, as if for blood. Although Stephen couldn't see any discernible difference in Belinda's face, he leant down and said, 'Are you okay?'

'Of course I'm not,' she snapped. She tilted her head back and closed her eyes, putting her fingers to her eye socket and pressing tenderly.

Chris returned with what appeared to be a white doctor's bag. It had the Belinda Burton's Naturaceuticals Therapeutic Day Spas logo—a light green leaf—on the side. He popped it open in a practised way and rummaged inside as Belinda looked on. He proffered a small jar and she wrenched it from him. 'Tea,' she said. Chris moved to the kettle.

Stephen said, 'Yeah, so, you know, I thought those empty shops in the Plaza could be a good spot for your—' and gestured at the bag with a corn chip.

Belinda turned slowly to face him, her expression now pure contempt. Belinda Burton's Naturaceuticals, she told him, was an *iconic luxury brand*. She waited for that to sink in, and then said her Therapeutic Day Spas were located only in the most suitable *high-end* consumer destinations. She unscrewed the cap of the jar and dabbed her cheekbone with a strong-smelling ointment, wincing as she did so.

'Ah,' said Stephen, chastened. 'Sorry. Thought you were expanding.'

'I am *expanding*,' Belinda spat. 'But I have to be very careful with the *guardianship* of my *brand*.'

'Oh. Right.'

Chris came to Belinda with a cup and saucer. She accepted it with a quick, tiny nod of her head as if it were an overdue apology, and he put it on the table.

'I should see if I can help Fiona,' said Stephen. Chris and Belinda watched him make his way out of the room. As he walked down the hall he heard Belinda's voice hissing in disbelief: '. . . the little bogan slappers of *Norton!*'

But in the hallway Stephen met Fiona's father carrying a laundry basket full of supermarket shopping in plastic bags, and Stephen had no choice but to step quickly backwards into the kitchen, propelled by the unstoppable force of Pat and his basket.

Pat was a large, brick-shaped man whose central occupation was the maintenance of his physical health. He and Jeanette, scurrying behind him, made a neat, compact couple, as if he had chosen her for the fact that her body might fit neatly inside the frame of his own. They were like stackable Tupperware. When Pat was feeling affectionate he would refer to Jeanette as his *little mate*, but this was rare. Mostly he simply barked orders at her and distanced himself from her foolishness by pointing it out to others.

Today Pat wore a navy-blue t-shirt that said PARIS—NEW YORK—ROME—PEPPERMINT BEACH in white lettering on his chest. The t-shirt was tucked into spotless ironed jeans, and Stephen noticed once again that there was no sign of belly overhang at the plaited leather belt. On seeing Pat, Stephen had instinctively sucked his own gut in, but after a few moments had to let it out again. Pat wore polished tan boat shoes with black leather tassles, and tennis socks. He and Jeanette lived at Peppermint Beach. They called the suburb *Peppy*. Pat often reminded people that he was a life member of the Peppermint Beach Chamber of Commerce.

He lowered the laundry basket on to the bench and nodded at Stephen without smiling. He called out 'Hello sweetheart,' to Belinda and strode across the room to kiss her. She winced.

Pat turned to Chris. 'Whatsamatter?' He was not in the habit of speaking directly to women when something mattered.

'He kicked me,' Belinda said in a small voice.

'What!' Pat turned, aghast, to glare at Stephen.

Chris said, 'Not him, Dad. Aleksander. *Accidentally*,' he added hurriedly.

'Uh,' said Pat, disappointed. He turned to look for Aleksander. They had all forgotten the baby for the moment.

'He's over there,' Stephen said. The baby swayed beside the modular metal bookcase where Fiona kept recipe books and the telephone. Aleksander had hauled himself upright, and for some minutes been supporting his wobbling weight not only by gripping the wire frame with both pudgy hands, but by latching his mouth on to a small nipple-shaped bolt protruding from the end of a shelf. He stood, happily anchored by the vacuum force of his suck.

'Oh my God!' cried Belinda, glaring at Stephen and then catapulting across the room and prising her little finger into Aleksander's mouth to release its seal from around the bolt. 'That's dirty! Chemicals! Dirty!'

She batted roughly at Aleksander's lips as she swept him into her arms, and then mouthed something at Chris that Stephen couldn't make out as she rushed to the sink and leaned over it, turning the tap on full.

'It doesn't look *that* dirty,' Stephen said mildly. He was a little offended on Fiona's behalf, but mainly felt sorry for Aleksander. He remembered with a clear sensual pleasure the illicit tastes from his own childhood: the chill, salty, gratifyingly oily taste of metal or the sour, lemony wood of the mahogany pew in Mass. You could run your tongue along the grooves in the soft wood made by other children's fingernails, bite secretly into it to leave tiny, satisfying marks.

Aleksander was subjected to a mouth-hosing at the sink which he bore without complaint, only curving out of his mother's arms now and then to look longingly toward the metal shelves.

Stephen shouldn't have said anything. Aleksander's quiet diligence at the shelves was one of the things he admired about children. Their silent dedication to tasks that nobody else found interesting, or necessary, but to which they could devote long, happy hours of improvement. It seemed an adult preoccupation to stop them from completing these tasks, but children understood their pleasure, and so did Stephen. Last week he had phoned and Ella answered, and they chatted amiably. 'What are you up to?' he'd asked her.

She'd sighed. 'Well,' she said, 'I'm *trying* to stick these tissues together. But it's not working very good.'

'What are you sticking them with?'

'Just spit,' she said.

'Oh,' said Stephen. 'And what about Larry?'

There was a pause. He pictured Ella walking about the house with the phone tucked beneath her chin. He listened to the congested snuffle of her breath into the phone as she walked, and felt a stab of love. 'Ah yeah,' Ella said then. 'She's in Mum's room cutting up a banana skin wiv' scissors.'

When Larry was small Fiona had once found her in the kitchen, working her way around the room with the pastry brush, diligently and thoroughly painting each lower cupboard door with margarine.

But now Stephen recalled the girls' faces hardening against him earlier. He would never again speak to them on the phone, never be allowed these glimpses of their private lives, their inventiveness, the intricacy of their minds.

He really needed a drink.

A horde of girls in fairy costumes came whirling through the kitchen, squealing and giggling, Ella at its centre, Larry bringing up the rear. A stray, wan little boy in a wizard's hat, anxious and dreamy-looking, bumped along in the middle of their swarm. Aleksander yelped, and then began to cry. Belinda held him struggling in her arms until the children had run out through the glass doors and then, exasperated, let him down to the floor.

She crouched down then, saying into his blank little face, 'Don't touch dirty things! Okay? Mummy said *no dirty!*'

He smiled at her and fell down on his soft, padded bottom.

The kitchen grew crowded. Jeanette stood washing her hands at the kitchen sink. Whenever Jeanette arrived anywhere she could be found washing her hands at the kitchen sink, and then obsessively folding and refolding a tea towel. Fiona, too, had finally reappeared, ushering the morose-looking mother of one of the children into the kitchen before her.

'This is Maureen, everybody—Joshua's mum,' called Fiona. 'Can somebody get her a cold drink or a cup of tea or something? I have to go talk to the fairy.' As she left the room Fiona raised her eyebrows at Stephen. Her rueful smile said *it will all be over soon.*

The woman Maureen stood in the middle of the kitchen, pale and aimless as her son.

'Hello, love,' Jeanette sang to Maureen, the kettle in her raised left hand. Stephen saw the wiry length of Jeanette's bicep muscle slide back and forth beneath the slack skin as she filled the kettle and plugged it in. She and Pat both exercised daily as if their lives depended on it, striding the suburbs in baseball caps and gigantic athlete's shoes. Stephen supposed their lives did depend on it.

His mother in Rundle came to him again. Sweating before the television screen, the greying, once-velour tracksuit pants from 1989 stretched across the broad beam of her bum as she pounded away on her Wii Fit, whatever it was. The idea of his mother sweating upset him. What if she had a heart attack, sweating on her machine? What if it happened today? His last words to her had been curt and cruel.

The afternoon sun was boring in through the kitchen windows, making the room even hotter. Stephen pulled his t-shirt away from his body. The rancid oil reeked up at him again. Was he the only one sweating like a pig? He looked around. Jeanette, despite her general nerviness, appeared never to perspire. She competed in the seniors section of the Peppermint To Pier half-marathon every year, and once Stephen went with Fiona to pick her up at the end. Apart from a rosy, excitable expression and prattling even more than usual, she seemed completely unaffected by the run. Stephen was astounded.

Today Jeanette wore a watermelon-coloured top with short petal-like sleeves and soft frills down the front. The top billowed, yet somehow still showed Jeanette's figure as slender. She wore white cropped jeans that emphasised the slim uniformity of her legs, and white sandals on her tanned, bony feet. On her fingers were the four or five gold and jewelled rings she always wore, and a heavy gold chain hung around her neck. Stephen sometimes wished his own mother would wear clothes like Jeanette's, instead of the blotchy floral blouses and roomy, elastic-waisted navy pants she had worn since his childhood. But Margaret would find herself ridiculous in such clothes. *Far too young*, she would say. Which was why she had always looked old.

Belinda said, 'You look nice, Jeanette.'

'Oh! The blouse is Country Road,' Jeanette said, pointing a skinny forefinger at her bosom and then, looking to the ceiling so as not to be distracted, began counting off the rest of her outfit on her fingers: 'The pant is from Sportscraft, and—' frowning down through the lattice of her fingers at her shoes, 'Oh! Esprit! Just cheapies, but I thought they were fun!' And she lifted a heel coquettishly, then giggled and gave her pillowy blonde hair a little shake.

Pat rummaged among the bags with his great hands, while Jeanette turned back to the bench, and stood up on her tiptoes to reach for coffee cups in the cupboard above his head. Maureen stood, hands empty by her sides, her boiled-vegetable-coloured dress drooping to her sandalled feet.

Stephen felt sorry for Maureen but his intent was focused on a gradual, casual move toward the fridge and a beer. Now he was there, his hand on the door, he noticed for the first time in months a drawing of Ella's among the notes and papers and drawings. It was from way back at the start of the year, and the photocopied lettering at the top said *My Aussie Mum*. Beneath that was Ella's awkwardly composed picture of a fat round woman in a flowered dress. In the teacher's neat hand in purple texta below the picture were the dictated words: *My Aussie Mum. She wears skirts. She wears dresses. She has brown hair.* The evening of the day she brought it home, Fiona and Stephen had passed the picture back and forth to one another and laughed till they wiped tears away. Australia Day had a lot to answer for. Fiona rarely wore anything but jeans.

Now Stephen stared at the picture, remembering how pleased he had been that there was no accompanying *My Aussie Dad*.

Why had he never had children of his own? Here in the kitchen, for the first time in his life, the question came to him, bald and shocking.

He glanced into the living room for Fiona, but she was not there. He opened the fridge and reached in for a bottle of Heineken.

He could see down the length of the hallway and out into the bright front yard from here. Fiona was at the gate, calling to the kids that the fairy was arriving. The house filled with a dozen ear-splitting screams and the girls came galloping through the kitchen once more. Joshua squealed along with the rest of them, but seemed not to know what it was he squealed about. From the living room ABBA's 'Waterloo' exploded.

Stephen looked at the clock. It was four-thirty.

'Like a beer, Pat?' called Stephen over the noise, as indifferently as possible, sliding a bottle along the bench. 'What about you, Maureen? Glass of wine? Beer?'

Maureen looked down at the cup in her hand and then at Jeanette.

'She's got a cuppa *tea*,' said Jeanette witheringly.

Pat shook his head in agreement at Stephen's stupidity, but he took the beer anyway and turned back to showing Chris his mobile phone. 'And look at this. Compass.'

Then Jeanette cried suddenly, 'All my life I've wanted a life-sized Alice chess set!' The others turned to look at her.

'For Pete's sake,' growled Pat, and sniffed a long, liquid snort. Stephen, watching Pat's laboured swallow of what had gathered in his throat, felt nauseous. He took a large swig from his beer, and for a moment was gloriously lost in the draught of it, the deliciously cold pins of it over his tongue, all down his throat. He put the bottle to his forehead. He saw that Aleksander had got up again and, unobserved by the others, was stepping unsteadily toward the living room door.

Jeanette ignored her husband, looking down at her splayed fingers, smiling slyly. 'I don't need your permission,' she sang gaily to her rings, and then beamed around the room, finally resting her triumphant gaze upon the toaster.

'Your mother's got a pretty face but she can be a silly bitch,' Pat said to Chris.

'Dad,' said Chris.

Stephen watched Aleksander's progress toward freedom. As the baby reached the door, he spied a peanut-half on the floor. With sudden speed and agility he dropped to all fours, plucked the peanut up, pushed it into his right ear and crawled off into the living room. Stephen suppressed an urge to cheer.

Pat ignored his son and locked eyes with Belinda. 'Sorry, love. But the woman's got no idea. I've told her that.'

Belinda only winced, still dabbing at her cheekbone with the ointment.

'They make the chess sets in Germany,' Jeanette said to Maureen, who nodded vigorously, terrified by the looming argument. Jeanette began smoothing her trousers and said with pride, 'Danka found out for me.'

Danka was Jeanette's boss in the expensive bed-linen store in the Peppermint Beach Village shopping strip where she worked one day a week. The shop was called Blue Duck Green, or White Bird Blue, or some other name to do with birds and unrelated to bed linen. Jeanette and Danka's shared passions included mohair throws and Nigella Lawson. Jeanette did not need to work but loved going to the shop, which she called Duckys or Bluey or Birdy. She had baby nicknames for everything. Her red Audi was called Ruby. I'm just taking Ruby for a run down to Peppy.

Jeanette said proudly that Danka had found the chess set on a website. Pat stood by shaking his head, arms folded. The internet had changed everything for Jeanette, as it had for Stephen's mother. There was nothing these women could not do now. If they didn't know something, they found a chat site and asked someone. If they wanted to buy a wig or a giant chess set or a Wii Fit or a trip to Santiago de Compostela, off they went. This was what sent Pat rigid with fury. Having prided himself on always telling people his wife could have whatever she wanted, now that she could actually *get* whatever she wanted under her own steam, he was a tyrant deposed.

Stephen's own father would have greeted Margaret's technological love affair with alarm, too. If his father had lived she wouldn't have had a chance at it. But it wasn't just the internet for Margaret—she didn't even have a credit card until he died. Jeanette, on the other hand, had always been canny with a credit card, and now she had the job with computer access at Danka's, the world of internet shopping was her oyster.

'She doesn't even know how to play chess!' Pat shouted, braying one of his nastier laughs. He shook his head slowly at Belinda to make her agree with him: 'Chess set. For *outside*. Jesus bloody wept.'

'It's already ordered!' Jeanette's eyes shone at Stephen, but then she remembered he was irrelevant so—seeing Belinda was already taken—she turned to engage Maureen in the wonders of the chess set's workmanship.

'It's available stained or *beautifully hand-painted*—I chose hand-painted, in blue and red,' she said. 'The pieces are all hand-carved, easy to lift. The queen is Alice, the bishops are Mad Hatters and the pawns are White Rabbits.'

She turned to stare out through Fiona's glass doors, perhaps imagining the chess pieces out there on the terrace.

Pat said to Belinda, 'I dunno where the bloody hell she thinks it's gunna go.' Jeanette might have won the battle but the war was far from over.

Jeanette whirled around to Belinda. 'By the pool! I told him! There's plenty of room by the pool!'

'Ha! It's not even *level* down there. I told her! I said, go for your life! Your bloody White Rabbits can all roll down the bank!'

Pat was enjoying himself now, chuckling at Maureen who stood there, silent and moist-eyed. She looked very tired. She was sallow and flat-chested in her sad, boring dress with the gaping armholes. Nobody had offered her a seat and she was too timid to take one.

'Why don't you take a load off, Maureen,' Stephen said, gesturing to the bench at the bay window. She almost smiled at him, and then backed away to the seat.

Chris came to stand beside Stephen. Quietly so Belinda could not hear he said, 'So you're heading up to Rundle next weekend? Say hi to your mum for me.'

He said it casually, but Stephen's heart lurched in his chest. How could Chris know about this? And why would he bring it up now?

'Um, yeah, well I don't know if that's still on, actually,' he murmured.

But Chris looked surprised. 'Oh I thought it was. I spoke to Cathy earlier,' he said.

A new wave of heat flushed horribly through Stephen's body. He felt a trickle of sweat creeping deep into his ear. Did Chris know? When did he talk to Cathy? Was he pretending surprise, had she told him—surely not—about Fiona?

'Right,' he said. He could not meet Chris's eye again.

Belinda called to Chris then, pointing at the stroller. She wanted it put away.

Stephen seized the moment, took his beer into the living room. The children had disappeared out to the garden with the fairy, and he stood in the blissful, carpeted silence. Children's things were strewn everywhere: a sparkling gumboot, two pairs of wings, a striped pair of damp knickers that someone had discarded, a red hairclip, a half-eaten piece of iced donut.

Aleksander stood beneath the window, gripping another bookshelf with one hand and peaceably pulling tissues from a box with the other. They rose in a soft white cloud at his feet. Stephen sat down cross-legged beside him, put his beer on the shelf and pulled the baby gently into his lap, tipping him sideways until the peanut fell out. Aleksander gave him a puzzled look, but didn't protest. Stephen smelt his head and kissed it before propping the baby back up at the bookshelf. 'All yours, buddy,' he said, standing him before the tissue box. Aleksander frowned, and returned to his work.

Stephen stood up, sucked again at the beer bottle. He felt lightheaded from standing too suddenly, or the beer, or the heat. Or guilt. He put out his hand on the window-sill to steady himself.

Outside, Larry and two of the little girls squatted in their fairy clothes before the drooping leaves of a shrub. In the gloom beneath the canopy Stephen could see the dim white face of Fluffy, the rabbit. Larry thrust her arm into the darkness and hauled the scrabbling creature out into her lap; the girls squealed with disgusted delight. But then the rabbit convulsed and wrenched free, and darted back beneath the bush, too far for Larry to reach. 'Good for you, bunny,' Stephen whispered. Stay there, and don't come out.

At the front door he heard a heavy step, and Richard's voice.

CHAPTER 5

'So who organised the lesbian?'

Belinda snickered into her mineral water as Richard bent to kiss her hello. As he straightened, she clasped his forearm to inspect his watch.

'Is that the new Panerai?'

Richard nodded, and shook his wrist. Belinda called, 'Chris, you should get a Panerai. They're top of the line.' She gave Richard, a wide, appreciative smile. They didn't take their eyes off each other.

From several paces away the watch looked just like

Stephen's father's old one from the fifties. He supposed that was the point. He supposed it cost a million dollars. Belinda never even smiled at Chris the way she did now at Richard, but then Chris probably didn't know what a Panerai was any more than Stephen did. Richard and Belinda should get a room. A schoolboy's snigger bubbled up inside him.

Richard surveyed the room from his great height, nodding at Maureen before striding across the floor to greet Jeanette and Pat with the same warmth he had Belinda. He ignored Stephen altogether. Stephen pretended not to notice, and drained his beer. He wanted another one, right now.

Jeanette tittered. 'Richard! That's not very kind! She's not a lesbian, she's a fairy.'

Pat roared from the corner at his wife's unintentional gag. Jeanette giggled again and batted Pat's silliness away with her hand. 'I mean her *daughter* is a fairy, but she's got gastro. That one's an ambulance lady, apparently.'

'Huh,' Richard said. This was the way Richard ended conversations. Huh. Whatever. Stephen felt acid squirling through his gut.

They all turned to look through the French doors, past the deck, where the fairy could be seen squatting on her thick thighs on the lawn, the wings straining across her back. She had a purple blanket spread out before her and was slowly rotating the plastic wand in the air—the way a riot policeman might threaten with a baton. She shouted at the children in her rasping voice. The little girls and Joshua sat before her as instructed, cross-legged, backs straight, staring up at her in hopeful horror, their gazes flicking often to the pink velour sack she had beside her.

Stephen drew back from the window. He must keep himself out of her sight. He realised his jaw had been clenched tightly shut ever since Richard arrived. He opened his mouth wide, made his ears click. This was quite possibly the longest day he had ever lived. He saw the junkie girl flying through the air. Smack, on the bitumen. Huh. Junkie. *Smack.* He stopped a high weird laugh beginning in his throat.

He had to get a grip.

He took command of himself, marching to the fridge. But somehow, in a single smooth movement Richard got there first, reaching in and taking a beer from the six-pack—Stephen's six-pack—all the while keeping his gaze on Stephen. Richard flipped the fridge door; it closed with a soft sucking sound. He levered off the cap with an opener and put the Heineken bottle to his mouth, fondling the cap in his other hand. Stephen dangled his empty bottle. He could not be sure that Richard wasn't smiling as he drank.

Richard swallowed, still watching him. Then he said, with exaggerated politeness, 'Would you like a *drink*, mate? Let me get you one.' And he reached inside the fridge again, took out one of Stephen's beers, and handed it to him in his great footballer's mitt. Stephen had to pull slightly to take the bottle from Richard's grasp.

'You alright, mate? You look a bit stressed.' Richard flicked his eyes over Stephen's sweaty clothes. Once more Stephen had the feeling Richard knew things about him.

But who cared, he chided himself. Who cared what this fucking Neanderthal thought of him? Richard was an oaf. Words like this were comforting: *boor*. *Lout*. But today they were not enough, faced as he was now with the expensive suit, the knowing, malevolent smile. The fancy watch around the thick, tanned, hairless wrist. The *size* of the man. Even the features of Richard's face were aggressive: slightly bulging, almost lashless eyes, the way the flesh of his face pressed outwards against the skin. The nose, broken in some long ago enactment of violence—rugby, or a college punch-up—healed, but left crooked as a reminder of what he might be capable of. His dark furze of hair, soldier-short to show the severe, perfectly symmetrical arches of his widow's peak. When he was silent his chin jutted, his lips pressed firmly shut. Richard had learned the power of keeping silent, while his cold, surveying eyes took everything in. Stephen hated his guts.

'I'm fine thanks,' he said, prising the lid off the beer and walking away, swallowing a long cold draught of the drink. For these remaining hours, he knew now, only beer would save him. He went over to Maureen, and asked her how old her kid was. She answered, and then began to speak about her husband, but Stephen did not listen. He watched Richard taking possession of the room.

Richard and Belinda began chatting about the all-ordinaries, and then about something Stephen couldn't hear. Belinda laughed out loud and then stifled it. She glanced at Stephen and then back to Richard, who was grinning nastily.

Stephen wished he had never bought the fucking Aldi trousers.

Belinda whispered something else to Richard. They were no longer smirking. Richard stood up again, shaking his head slowly in a disgusted way. Stephen turned away from watching them—he was being paranoid, he knew. Those two always made him feel like this.

He drained his beer and looked around the room.

Maureen had drifted away, and Pat now had her bailed up in the corner. She sipped her tea and nodded in weary silence under the barrage of his voice. He was sick of all the people coming to this country who thought Australia owed them a living. Did she know what he meant? Now and then Maureen sent a fretful glance through the window.

The paramedic fairy had the children arranging themselves on the purple blanket for pass-the-parcel. She had a battered black ghetto blaster next to her on the grass, its handle wound with pink tinsel. The little boy Joshua, the crumpled wizard's hat slipping sideways and its shiny green elastic tight at his pale throat, sat neatly on his knees at the edge of the group of the girls. Ella's crisp, arch voice soared over all. She pointed, flung orders. 'You sit there, Jessica. Sophie: next to me. Joshua—*move!*' She shoved him. Her cheeks were highly coloured, her lips wet. But the other children seemed to accept her reign without question. It was Ella's house, and Ella's birthday. Joshua, whose large, watchful eyes appeared permanently on the verge of tears, scrambled as he was bid; they all did. The little girls, apart from Ella and Larry, were virtually indistinguishable: all were head to toe in pink or purple, their soft hair fuzzing in the humidity, ribbons and hairclips slipping, sweaty tendrils plastering to their cheeks. They bickered and jostled, clambered about the blanket as directed. They were named Sage and Paris and Sophie and Emily and Taylor. Ella was the ruling force. They shouted commands, repeating her directives, pushed each other out of the way to obey them. If any child dissented she was rounded on by the others.

Stephen was horrified by Ella's tyranny, their obedience. Even Larry, who normally greeted Ella's orders with a sneer or silence, leapt to attention or fetched whatever Ella ordered. But Larry looked strange, too—both the girls did, with their too-bright eyes and red cheeks; their high, artificial laughter was weird in the air. They seemed to Stephen—he felt a stab—like someone else's children.

The fairy squatted by the CD player, and barked at them to get into a circle. 'Orright, *go*.'

The parcel crept from child to child, as if pushed through water. All eyes hungrily followed the parcel. Once a girl wrenched it from another's grasp into her lap, it moved glacially until it was torn from her grip. The fairy stood sweating above them, hands on her hips. She punched the ghetto blaster's buttons on and off with a fat big toe.

Charlotte Wood

The adults all gathered at the doorway now to watch. Each time the music stopped, a present fell from the wrapping and the child scrabbled to catch it. Pat snorted. 'Every bloody time, they get something these days. These kids'll never learn what the real world is like till it hits 'em between the eyes.'

Nobody responded except polite Maureen, who began to signal a mild disagreement by tilting her head, then gave up and nodded in assent.

'So what's your husband do?' Pat demanded. It would not occur to him to ask about a woman's work.

Fiona appeared at his side. 'Dad, could you help me get the seats organised for musical chairs?'

Pat looked suspicious, and nodded at Stephen. 'What about him, or is he too useless to pick up his own dick?' He had not been fooled. 'Whatsamatter with asking about 'er husband?'

Fiona smiled apologetically at Maureen and said, 'Eric's sick, Dad, so he's not working at the moment.'

Pat was filled with new enthusiasm. He turned back to Maureen. 'What, has he got cancer!'

Maureen nodded, blinking fast as her eyes filled. 'Dad,' begged Fiona. At the mention of cancer Chris turned

230

too, met Fiona's eye and then sent a look of sympathy Maureen's way.

'What stage?' said Pat. There was no way he was budging now.

A wail rose from the circle outside, and Fiona hurried towards the door. As she passed Stephen she glanced at his empty beer bottle. 'Can you do something to help?'

He was stung. 'Like what?'

'Like, anything! Save Maureen, for a start.' She shoved past him, out towards the wailing.

He looked across the room. If she was going to keep talking to Pat the woman would need a drink. He pulled a bottle of wine from the fridge door.

'Sixteen years ago I was diagnosed with prostate cancer,' Pat was announcing. 'I woke up out of me operation and I looked around at the other blokes and I thought, these people are my enemies.'

'Maureen?' Stephen urged her with his eyes to say yes to the bottle he held over a fresh glass, to come across the room to him and escape. But she shook her head, immobilised.

Stephen tried to interrupt Pat, gesturing with a beer bottle and the wine. 'Refill? Pat?'

Pat ignored him, deep in memory. 'I thought, I'm stuffed if that pansy crying over there's gunna beat me to the finish line.'

'So Maureen,' Stephen tried. 'Joshua's your little boy, is he?'

But Pat, whose voice did not falter, shifted a little to place himself between Maureen and Stephen, and went on. Stephen smiled helplessly at her; he had tried. All he could do was keep her company now. He filled the empty glass to the brim and took a big swig of the icy yellow wine.

'I thought, eff-you mate, excuse the French, darling.' Pat cleared his throat with the liquid snort again. 'I thought, you weak bastard. I thought, good! You go ahead, take the easy road out and die. Gives me more chance.'

Maureen reared back at this, eyes blinking fast. Stephen took another deep swallow of the cold wine. Why was it that when you most wanted to get drunk you remained most offensively sober? Through the open window came the sound of a helicopter. Stephen and Maureen turned to watch it, following the aircraft's effortless glide through the skies, away across the city.

'He's gotta stand up and *fight* it, darling, is what I'm saying.'

Outside the pass-the-parcel had disintegrated, the children had scattered and were coming back inside. Fiona bent over Ella, gripping her wrist, as they walked.

'But *I'm* the birthday girl!' she howled.

Behind them a girl called Amy squatted in her fairy skirt over the pass-the-parcel prize, a cheap imitation Barbie doll in a cellophane bag. Amy studied Fiona and Ella, the doll wedged firmly between her thighs in case Fiona might be unjustly swayed and come to claim it back.

Fiona steered Ella by the shoulders into the kitchen, calling over her noise, 'Listen, El, shush, in a minute we'll have the cake!'

Ella screamed as if stabbed: 'I don't *want* any *cake!*' The adults stopped talking and turned toward her. Fiona smiled ruefully at them and then turned back to speak to Ella in low, calming tones. But she was beginning to grow frantic, holding tight to her daughter's wrist, trying to protect her from the shame of her own bad behaviour. Now and then over Ella's head Fiona called to the little girl still crouched outside, 'It's okay, darling, it's your prize, nobody's going to take it,' only to raise another round of shrieks from Ella.

Stephen watched, pained. This panting, bellowing creature was not his girl, not thoughtful, telephone-snuffling

Ella. Her face was stained red from some lolly, her hair was damp and matted and the fairy skirt wrenched sideways. She snarled into her mother's face, alive with hatred, but also, Stephen saw, with fear. She was on a precipice; she needed rescuing.

Three girls stood by, captivated. One of them said ostentatiously, 'You can have my prize, Ella', and held out a plastic bangle. Ella lunged and screamed, flinging the bangle to the floor so it bounced and wheeled away.

'Ella!' shouted Fiona. The three girls began to smile slyly at each other, thrilled by this unravelling.

Fiona steered Ella, still howling, into the living room. The girls followed, riveted.

Stephen turned back to Pat and Maureen, the bottle still in his hand. Pat, who had not paused in his lecture but only raised his voice to compete with Ella's bellows, held out an empty glass to Stephen without looking at him. 'Nobody owes your husband anything, is what I'm saying, love. He wants to cure himself, he's gotta work at it like everything else in life.'

'For Christ's sake,' Stephen muttered, filling Pat's glass and then pouring the dregs of the bottle into his own.

'What's your problem?' Pat growled.

Stephen shook his head and gulped wine. 'Nothing.'

He was finally feeling something from the alcohol. At last. He felt his edges loosening. 'You were saying. Please continue. No free lunches, was it?'

Maureen looked at Stephen anxiously.

'What would you know about it?' sneered Pat. 'I didn't give in to my disease. I fought it.'

'You also had surgery and radiotherapy. So maybe medicine saved you,' Stephen said. He pulled at the neck of his t-shirt, trying to create a breeze. 'Or maybe you were just lucky.'

Pat's lip curled. 'This lady's husband is in deep shit, mate. *Deep* shit. I'm tryna help her keep him alive, you dickhead.'

'Please,' said Maureen. She looked as if she might be sick, or sink to the floor. Stephen felt the alcohol spreading all along his clenched spine, his jaw; he felt the blessed, liberating release of it.

'In that case, while you're at it, Pat, you better get Belinda on board,' he said. 'You see, cancer only kills you if you don't eliminate the *toxins*, Maureen.' He honked a laugh.

Belinda was looking at him, along with Chris and Richard.

'And,' Stephen said—sailing in the open now, how good it felt!—'Belinda reckons only control freaks get it anyway.

So your husband's getting what he deserves, see, but that can all be fixed if he pops along to one of Belinda's spas for a six-hundred-dollar frigging *coffee enema*.'

He turned to laugh in bitter sympathy with Maureen. But he saw then that she did not welcome his help. In fact she had begun to cry.

Pat took hold of Stephen's upper arm in a vicious grip, and hissed into his ear, 'You're a *stupid* little turd.' He turned back to the softly weeping Maureen, putting an arm around her shoulders. 'Come on darling, let's get you home.'

He could feel sweat on his eyelashes. He blinked. In the next room ABBA's 'Ring Ring' burst on and off for musical chairs; the children squealed and shrieked.

But the kitchen was silent. Stephen stood in the room, with everyone looking.

'What's the matter?' said Fiona, coming in with an armful of crumpled wrapping paper, staring around at them all. 'Where's Maureen?'

'I was just trying to,' Stephen said. His mouth was dry. He licked his lips, looking down the hallway, out into the front yard where Maureen and Pat stood by the front gate talking intently, Pat's hands grasping her shoulders. Maureen was nodding again, but now looking gratefully into Pat's eyes.

How had this happened?

'Pat was the one . . .' Stephen said. Plaintive as a child. But Belinda interrupted. 'Stephen seems to have upset Maureen by making a joke of her husband's cancer for some reason,' she said icily.

'Noo,' said Stephen in a faint voice. He was finding it difficult to stand, the air was so terribly, terribly hot.

'What?' Fiona was mystified. She looked at the glass in Stephen's hand. 'What is the matter with you?' She was genuinely confused. He was upsetting her. He saw that she was tired of protecting him. He could see in her face what she was asking: why must he do this, *in front of them?*

Stephen licked his lips again. 'I was—nothing. Forget it.'

He propelled himself from the room, down the hallway. He went into Fiona's bedroom and shut the door. The bed was made up, the white sheets flat and clean and bare. This was the place, his and Fiona's place, this cool dark room, with the heat beating down beyond the wooden blinds, where everything had opened up. This was what he wanted. He lay down on the bed, the sheet smooth, the pillow white against his cheek. He closed his eyes. How had he suddenly got so drunk?

Outside, beyond the window, came a low scrabbling noise. It was Fluffy, he thought, hiding just out there under the darkness of the orange blossom bush, silent, waiting them all out. *Fright or flight.* The animals knew, alright, and Stephen knew too. He lay in the blissful quiet. In his head Fluffy shifted in the gloom. Then he realised: *fight*, not fright. He sat up, smelling the rank oil on his skin. He would spoil Fiona's fresh, beautiful bed with his filthy clothes; he had left her out there, all by herself. He had to go back to the party. He could not—yet—abandon her.

It was fight or flight, and this was not his refuge anymore.

The kitchen table was crowded with children, their elbows slipping and sliding on the thin plastic tablecloth. The room was all primary colours and high, excitable babble. Through the window Stephen saw the fairy smoking a cigarette in the garden, her meaty arms folded. She blew the smoke downwards over the costume's wisps and petals into her great cleavage.

He went to the fridge and lifted out a jug, poured a glass of cold water and drank it down. He would pull himself together. He stared outside, across the water. If he was out there he could be free, stepping onto the ferry as it pulled away, putting the cool dark harbour between him and this day, this terrible mess of a day. He would stand on the ferry deck, the wind cool in his face. He could step off the boat and sink, an anchor or a stone, straight down into the black deep.

He dragged his attention to the table.

Ella was perched on a mass of cushions in the big chair at the head of the table. Now she had regained centre stage she had stopped her sobbing, but Stephen saw that the hysteria lay in her, shivering like water about to boil. She wore the purple glittery bangle she had earlier hurled to the ground; Fiona must have found the other girl a compensatory gift.

Ella knelt on her throne of cushions. She leaned with her palms flat on the table as she craned about, scanning the feast laid out before her, inspecting the other girls' places for evidence of anything she may have been denied. Joshua had gone, gathered up by his mother and Pat; the table was ringed now only with the pink- and purple-clad girls, chattering and giggling and jostling.

Ella paid them no heed. She was completely focused on the task at hand—she must account for all the things that were rightfully hers: the special plate, the cushions, the fullest cup, the prettiest paper hat, each girl sitting in exactly the place Ella decreed.

Jeanette bobbed around the table holding her camera in her outstretched hands, aiming at Ella. 'Smile for the photo, darling!' she called, hovering over the table, eyes fixed on the camera's screen. Ella turned to her and grinned a sickening false smile, squeezing up her cheeks and baring her teeth. All children did this now in the presence of cameras; it was expected of them. Photographs of children never really looked like them, but at least the images numbered in their thousands.

There was an exaggerated intake of breath from the adults as Fiona came carrying the cake, a massive pink-iced square covered in silver baubles and five striped candles. A murmur went up from the girls, and Richard led the singing of 'Happy Birthday', his rich courtroom voice heard above all others. Stephen stood in the corner, drinking his water.

Ella sat up straight among her cushions at the head of the table, beaming, finally, with genuine delight. Stephen exhaled; her composure was restored. She had reached the shore.

Then two of the girls, who earlier had been sweetly subservient, began to snicker, their heads together, while the singing carried on about them.

Happy Birthday to you. The girls fidgeted and giggled; one flicked a malicious grin Ella's way. Don't look, Stephen prayed—but she saw. She saw the tide turning. Her eyes widened in panic as she saw the girls' heads bent to each other in secret, laughing confidence. Stephen wanted to call out *it doesn't matter, they don't matter,* and take her in his arms. But Ella began to jiggle in her seat, her aggrieved gaze fixed on the faithless girls, desperate for their lost attention.

Happy Birthday dear Ellaaa.

The girls smirked, pushing sideways at each other, mocking Ella without even looking in her direction. This was the worst. She could not bear it—before the song finished she thrust herself bodily over the table, spat out the flames with wet breaths, then tore the candles from the cake and flung them into the air. The adults cried out and the children gasped, and Ella began to burrow into the cake with both her hands, clawing and shovelling clumps of it into her mouth, waggling her head, giggling shrilly at the traitorous pair, allowing cake to fall in sodden clods from her mouth.

'That's disgusting, Ella!' cried Jeanette. 'Stop it!' She leaned in to snatch the cake away. Now all the girls began squealing with horror and thrill while Ella pawed and smashed and dug, sending cake and clods of icing spinning. She drew herself up, chocolate dark as blood around her mouth, tick-tocking her crazed grin at the girls, shrieking in a high, lunatic voice: 'Look at me, *look at me!*'

All around her adult hands tried to catch the cake, reached in to save tilting drinks, and Ella jolted and screeched. And the girls laughed their dreadful mocking laughs.

Stephen could stand this no longer. He strode to the table and lifted Ella up and away. 'Let me *go*,' she screamed, writhing. The others watched as she clawed at him, convulsing and kicking, but he held her fast, carrying her across the kitchen, away through the next room, out of sight of them all.

In the hallway he set her down, crouched on the floor before her, breathless, gripping her firmly by the arms.

'Deep breaths, Ella,' he commanded, inhaling deeply himself, showing her. He would deliver her from this. He would banish this alien, degraded creature, restore her true nature, her sweet self-possession. But she wouldn't come with him; she howled and spat, twisting and heaving in his grip. 'Come on, Ellabella,' he called, low and calm, pressure building behind his eyes. 'Don't do this, shhh, shhh.' *Come on*, he willed her. *Please.* But she would not be subdued: she arched and spun and flailed, dragging in the breaths, gouging at him. Her face was blotched red and black with smeared chocolate, her hair sticky, one fairy wing torn and bent. 'I hate you,' she screeched, lips wet with rage. 'Stop it,' Stephen said, tightening his grip on her. 'Stop it.' Why could she not see that he alone understood? In desperation he began telling her things in a low, murmuring voice. He held her fast by the upper arms while she wrenched and roared, and he kept talking. He told her about when he was a little boy and went walking in the bush all by himself. About the twitching quiet and the fright of the occasional rustling leaves. He told her about the magpie that used to come to his bedroom window, how it would wipe its beak on the verandah rail, one side then the other as if it had a runny nose, how it would shiver its fat belly and the feathers there looked like fur. Ella still howled and lurched in his grip, but Stephen found he was calmed himself as he spoke. He held her firm and kept going, told how the magpie would jump with both feet up the steps, and it appeared the bird was jerked by invisible strings, like a puppet. Ella's shrieks began to stutter, to lose velocity. He talked about the puppet they had seen together at the Quay one day, and how she had learned to say *mar-i-on-ette*, that difficult word. She kept crying but she was listening now, her mournful eyes turned to him, snot everywhere. Please, he prayed. He would not let go, would not stop speaking. She drew a new breath to howl again, but the edge of hysteria had gone. He said remember the ferry, how she had sat on his lap in the great wind and how the water sprayed.

At last, her body began to soften; his grip on her shoulders softened too, and he could gently turn her to fall into his lap. Finally, finally, she stopped. He couldn't believe it. She shuddered in the silence, her face turned into his chest. They were both exhausted, but he had saved her. He prayed for this quiet to last as her halting breaths subsided, stroking her back in long, smooth strokes, not daring to stop talking about the ferry, how they had eaten chips they bought from the shop on the boat. She rested against him and he began to rock her with each stroke of her back.

There was a noise from the kitchen behind him. Jeanette bleated, and then he knew Richard was coming. He could feel the great body moving through the rooms. Please, he begged silently, let it not be ruined. Ella stayed where she was, surrendered, in his arms. But the hallway behind him filled with Richard's huge tread. It was imperative now for Stephen to hold this moment steady, keep Ella safe, save himself. He held her close with one arm as he twisted, gesturing behind him to show she had calmed down, batting away at Richard's enormous leaning bulk.

'She's fine now,' Stephen murmured, low and authoritative, to the shape of Richard, begging for the oaf to get it, to fuck off until Ella was strong and steady once again. He curved his body around the child's. But he could smell Richard's cool breath, the chemical wash of his body, his malice. He felt the floorboards move beneath the great approaching weight, felt the iron bar of Richard's knee pressing at his back.

'Come here,' Richard barked at Ella, his huge arms swooping down.

'She's settled now, she just needs a *minute*,' Stephen hissed over his shoulder, shuffling round in his crouch on the floor, shielding Ella, holding her tighter. She jerked, her breath rising into a whimper.

'Give her to me,' Richard ordered as he reached for Ella, the thick trunk of his arm grazing Stephen's ear, the elbow shoving at his cheek. Ella cried out, shrank into Stephen, clung to him. He would protect her. He pushed back against the force of Richard's great roving arm with his head, pushing and butting at it, like a goat.

'I said just *leave* her.'

Richard's forearm was pressed against Stephen's throat; the grasping hands took hold of Ella, who began to wail. Stephen held on.

'Let her go, you fucking loser,' Richard hissed into his ear.

And all the contempt the world had ever held for Stephen filled those last three words, and the great weight of this day swept up over him in a terrible wave, and crashed down. Just as Pat and the fairy opened the front door and appeared before them in the hall, Stephen sank his teeth deep into the flesh of Richard's smooth bare arm.

CHAPTER 6

The two men locked gazes in the swollen instant, and then Richard roared, 'Jesus fucking Christ!' Ella fell from Stephen's arms as Richard knocked him to the floor, and now she saw blood on her father's arm. *'Daddy!'* she cried, and lunged at Stephen, smacking at his face. Her father swept her up into his arms and ploughed back past Stephen to the kitchen. Pat followed, prancing along behind, shouting insults over his shoulder at Stephen. The fairy simply stood in the hallway, looking down at him with folded arms, shaking her head. 'You're completely insane,' she said, and then she stepped over him to follow the others into the kitchen.

Stephen knelt on all fours, staring, wild-eyed and lost, at the hallway floorboards. From the mesh of the day's disasters the dog in the newspaper photograph came to him, the animal who had mauled a child to death. Why had he done that? He was so tired. He wished only to lie down here in the narrow patch of space, but the little girls had all gathered to watch him from the living room. In the distant kitchen he saw the adults soothing Ella and Richard. The fairy stood inspecting Richard's arm.

Now Fiona stood above him with the staring, breathless children. She said, her voice full of fear, 'Stephen, please tell me what's wrong.'

He looked up at her. He swallowed. Then—oh no— Richard's frame filled the doorway once more. He pushed past Fiona, a sticking plaster covering the place on his arm where Stephen had bitten him.

'I've been very nice to you,' he spat.

'No you haven't!' cried Stephen, struggling to his feet.

'I've held my fucking tongue, I've done *nothing* to you up to this point. But that's it.' Stephen flinched, waited for it, the blow he had always known would come.

'Richard!' cried Fiona, putting herself between the two men. 'Just shut up. Go in the other room.'

But Stephen was the one who moved, full of adrenaline. He must find his bag and get out of here. He would phone Fiona, tell her later. Or never. He would never speak to her again. He shoved past Richard to the kitchen. Where was his bag? He began trotting around the room, scanning the floor and the bench and table for his bag, not meeting any of the eyes fixed upon him. But Richard followed his every step. Stephen dodged, looking under the table, by the window seat. The bag was not there. Richard towered over him. Stephen could smell his fury. Where was his *bag*?

'You're such a fucking loser,' Richard jeered. 'You've never had a proper job. You've never been married. Not even had a proper *girlfriend* from what I hear.' Stephen saw Chris looking at the floor. It didn't matter. He must find his bag.

It was Fiona's turn for rage. 'Shut up, Richard.' She rushed across the room, launching herself again at Richard, shouting, 'Just get out. Get out of my house.' She shoved at his immovable bulk.

'You don't own anything,' Richard went on. 'You don't have any kids. You wear bloody *chef's* pants. You call yourself an adult. And now you go around fucking *biting* people! What sort of animal are you?'

Stephen called out, 'Don't worry, Fi, I'm going.' He began wrenching at wrapping paper lying about, at newspapers. Where the fuck was his bag!

'You're not going, *he's* going!' cried Fiona, pointing at Richard. She turned to her ex-husband and held out her hands. 'Please.'

But Richard still followed as Stephen stumbled about the room. 'You've been messing my kids around for a year, coming and going whenever you want. Fiona's always forgiving you this and defending that, propping up your useless fucking life.'

Stephen's body was all adrenaline and nausea; he was afraid, more than anything, that he would sob, bawl like a child in front of them all. He tried to block out Richard's voice. He must find the bag. He opened a cupboard. This was ridiculous. *Where was it?*

'Your whole life is a failure,' Richard said then, calm and certain, like drawing out a splinter.

Stephen halted. The tears came, unstoppable.

'He's right,' Pat snarled from the corner of the room.

Stephen said stiffly, 'I can't find my bag.' Where, where on earth was it?

'And now,' Richard began to laugh dreadfully; a punch-line was coming: 'And now, the greatest fucking irony of all—Fiona should have gotten rid of you a year ago, and yet here you are, and now *you're* the one who's dumping *her!*'

Stephen stared at Richard, breathing fast. Belinda looked on, triumphant.

'*What?*' Fiona said.

Chris still stared only at the floor. So he had known, and told.

Stephen forced himself to turn, to meet Fiona's eyes. The room shrank to hold only her astonishment, this savage truth. He saw confusion ripple through her, saw her scan the room for protection, find none. She stared at him in disbelief. He couldn't say a word.

Richard said to him with final satisfaction, 'I could see it in your *face*, you little prick.' He threw Stephen's backpack from his own shoulder to the floor, and batted Fiona roughly on the back as she stood with tears streaming down her face in her own kitchen, watched by her parents and Chris and Belinda and all the children.

Stephen hauled his bag to himself, delved into it for his wallet. He was battered, ancient. His fingers came to the hard edges of the forgotten My Little Pony; he drew it out by a corner and hoisted the bag slowly to his shoulder.

He stepped across the room to where Ella was cradled by her grandmother, her face pushed into Jeanette's bony, bejewelled neck. Jeanette shrank back as he approached, as if Stephen might attack her. He bent down and put the toy on the table in front of them.

'I'm sorry, Ellabella,' he whispered, his voice catching. He spoke as near to her face as he could without touching her, without frightening her. He couldn't look in Fiona's direction. He wiped his hands on his trousers and walked from the room. He knew she was following him as he walked down the hallway, through the front door and out into the blistering heat.

At the gate he stopped. Fiona stood behind him, alone on the path. All the humming energy of her had drained away; she looked drab, dishevelled. He had done this.

'I don't understand,' she said. 'You're just going to leave me here, with all of them.'

She tried to collect herself. 'I don't understand what's even gone *wrong*,' she whispered. And suddenly she was just like Ella, wiping her wet nose with the side of her hand, unguarded as a child, her face blotchy with tears. He had done this; it was unbearable.

He said, 'I'm sorry. I just—'

He could find not a single thing more to say. *I just want to be free.* He could not say those stupid words. They had already withered in his mind, turned to dust. He did not even know, he marvelled now, what the hell those words had meant.

Fiona looked back towards the house, trying to compose herself. She drew in a single, shuddering breath, and exhaled. A corner of her mouth began pulsing, a tiny tremor. Then she said, still looking towards the house, 'You think I want what they tell me to. But when I think of them all in there, in that house . . .'

Ella and Larry appeared, began to clamber down the steps of the house. Fiona lifted her head and looked into his eyes. 'The only time I have ever felt that I could—' she searched for words—'properly *breathe*, is with you.'

Her eyes filled again, and as the girls reached her, winding themselves around her waist, the tears ran down her face. Her hands went to her daughters' heads as she struggled to stop crying. It was intolerable. Stephen was still frightening all of them, his girls. Ella stood in her limp fairy skirt and her dirty, twisted Barbie t-shirt. Larry watched on, frightened. Ella opened her mouth to speak. 'Are we still going to the circus?' she croaked.

He stared at her sticky, swollen face. 'I don't think so, Bella.' She stared back at him, still afraid, but did not cry.

'I have to go,' he whispered, and turned out of the gate. Walk.

He pushed his legs, they crossed one wide driveway, then another and another, the fences of the houses of Longley Point sliding past him. His head burned, his feet. His mouth was full of ash. His body was old and rank, polluted. He stared ahead to the tunnel of trees, the shade, then the bus stop: all he had to do was reach the stop. He entered the great shaded hollow made by the trees, and reached the bus shelter. He sat down on the metal strips of the seat and waited. He was free, and in the dark cool air and his sweat, he shivered.

CHAPTER 7

He lifted his head from the bus window as at long last it rounded the corner onto Park Road. He would soon be home to his empty, dirty house. To his bed, the snarled sheets velvety with grime. There were few passengers left on the bus. Two old women from the housing commission flats greeted each other from far seats, shouted about the heat, god jesus could they believe this weather, where was the promised cool change? One called that she had been on an errand for her grandson. 'He asked me to get him summa that Lynx,' she called.

'What?' said the other woman. 'What'd he want?'

The first woman rummaged in her plastic bags. 'That Lynx,' she said, brandishing the tall black can of men's deodorant. 'It's on special,' she said, and stroked the can before putting it away. It tinked against other cans in the bag.

Stephen thought dully of the grandson, what kind of grandson this might be. He remembered the Lebanese boy from the bus this morning. HARDEN THE FUCK UP, and now he saw the boy for what he was—the kind of boy who might be a grandson watching a television advertisement glistening with women's bodies, who saw a catalogue of supermarket specials and asked his grandmother to buy him some of that Lynx, and in her kindness she would do it, would go out into the ferocious heat of the city and fetch him the foolish thing. Because she loved him.

Margaret, his mother, had asked him for one simple thing, and he could not oblige her, because it was too much. He loved her; he would always hurt her. Poor creature. The grandmother smiled down into her shopping bags, and then waved to her friend as she lumbered towards the door, swaying in the intolerable air.

A group of people was gathered in a circle in Dunmore Park. As Stephen neared them he heard a strange hooting. It was the Laughing Club. A tall, pasty man with thinning blond hair, a purple yin-yang t-shirt and stew-coloured hemp shorts was its leader. He was grinning from ear to ear as he called to the small band of followers.

'Okay, fantastic. Fant*astic* chuckling. I'm really impressed with how you're doing, okay? And what I want to hear from you now is a big, raucous belly laugh.'

The people—a couple of middle-aged white women, a young Indian man Stephen recognised from the checkouts of the supermarket and two other scrawny, hippie-looking men who looked as if they might work in a health food shop—placed their hands on their stomachs. The leader began to tilt backwards and forwards from the hips, hands on the little pot of his belly, fingers spread wide. Stephen could not look away as the man called out, 'Ha! Ha! Ha!', seesawing forward and back in a parody of laughter. The others followed suit, barking out *hah*-has and hoh-hoh-hohs. The heat had not subsided, not even here in the green of the park. Stephen walked on, transfixed by this sad performance. Why were they not ashamed, to be doing this? He glanced up once more at one of the women, at her anxious eyes, her teeth bared at the leader as her mouth opened to let out the hollow sound, and then he was past them.

Stephen almost thought of relating this scene to Fiona—but he veered from the thought at the last instant, made his mind blank. His teeth ached, his mouth was dry. It was as though every drop of moisture from inside his body lay on his skin; his entire body was drenched in sweat.

He reached the corner of his street. The fake laughter filled the air behind him, only now it didn't sound so pathetic. Stephen was nudged by some understanding that had surfaced and subsided around him all day. It had to do with the *Big Issue* woman, and the junkie Skye. It was to do with the woman with the Sydney Olympics cord around her neck. It had to do with the Facebook girls, and the seals at the zoo, even Russell's surrender. It had to do—impossibly—even with Belinda, at the mercy of her beliefs, and Jeanette's sad attempts to stand up to Pat.

He had felt sorry for them all. But he had *left* Fiona and the girls. He had lost them. It came tumbling in: it was he, Stephen, who had been wretched all along. He was the lost one, the poor creature. Back in the park the laughter grew into hoots and shrieks. They were laughing now, actually laughing. It was Stephen who was alone and mirthless, coming to his empty house at the end of this dreadful, dreadful day.

Balzac, the German shepherd, appeared on the footpath in front of Stephen. Too tired to hold the dog's probing snout at bay, he simply kept walking as Balzac gave him a weary sniff. But Balzac was exhausted too, Stephen saw, watching the dog pant, his shaggy flesh rolling from side to side over his ribcage as he trotted alongside him. They neared Nerida's house. The house was empty, gate and front door shut with the locked-up look that only came with absence. From some way behind them a car came roaring along the street. As Stephen turned toward the noise he heard Balzac's claws scrabble on cement, heard the throat-deep growl as the dog leapt. Stephen cried out and lunged to grasp him but too late, and then it came, the skidding, the bang and Balzac's discordant yelp. The driver, a man, shouted 'DUMB FUCKING ANIMAL' and the car smoked off and away down the street.

In the road lay Balzac, shrugging and turning his long shaggy body on the bitumen, a yairling whine rising up out of him.

Stephen moved towards the fallen animal as if wading through thigh-deep water. For the second time today he knelt in the road, and he recognised this: in its leaping the dog, like the girl—like Stephen, too—had cast itself out. He knew the fatal impulse; he felt it in the animal, in his own body, as it leapt. He knelt beside the dog. He knew Nerida and Jill were not home, was grateful, for they must be protected from this sight: Balzac lying oddly bent, his front legs splayed, head slid sideways in pain on the bitumen, the long body dragging, breath whining out in a long, high, agonised hiss. His back was broken. Stephen put his hand to the soft heaving flank, concave beneath the ribs, then touched the dog's muzzle in a single strong, gentle stroke.

'Poor Balzac, poor boy.'

The dog's belly rose and fell, his head fallen still. '*Poor creature, poor boy,*' Stephen repeated, blinking to keep out the filaments of dusty hair rising into his eyes and mouth and nose. But he saw the animal's fearful brown eyes. Was it true, that animals did not foresee their deaths? If it was true, why did Stephen now recall his own father's eyes, cast around at them all, this same sorrowful stare, in the instant before he died?

He abandoned himself to the dog, to its gaze. He lay down on the road, his head on the bitumen, face turned to Balzac's, whispering *poor boy*, letting his eyes sting and his nose run. The dog panted, saliva hanging from his crinkled, leathery lips, his loosened tongue drooping. His breath came in short, shallow pants, and Stephen lay curved around him on the hot road, stroking the matted fur, smelling the warm piss steaming off the asphalt. This mess and agony. It was a life, ending, he marvelled, just as he was beginning to understand. The point of an animal was not for it to love you; it was that you could love it. In all its otherness, your unbelonging to its kind, it could yet receive—boundlessly—your love. He inhaled the dank animal breaths with his own, and he thought of his father, of his mother, how one day soon this dying gaze would be hers, endless and sorrowful. *Poor creature.* His own death would come, soon or distant, it didn't matter now. The animal's flanks rose and fell, rose and fell. His father's last shallow breaths became the dog's, there on the steaming road.

It was in this abjection, he saw now—his eyes closed, face pressed into the dog's neck—that we were most animal and because of that became most human after all. We all are only hair and bone and stinking breath, and the only thing we can hope for is a fellow creature who will lie beside us in the road, and stroke our flanks while we die.

He lay, stroking Balzac's life away with the exhausted, huffing little breaths. He opened his eyes and followed the line of the dog's slowing gaze. And he saw there a woman stepping from her car further up the street.

It was Fiona, shutting her car door, here in his street.

Stephen began to weep softly to the dog, to himself. She was here. He cried, gumming the hair with his snot and tears, and another door opened and Ella and Larry climbed out. Stephen lay weeping and they stepped off the kerb and came to sit down beside him and the dog in the road. Fiona put out her hand to the rising, falling fur, and whispered, *Poor boy, we're here.*

ACKNOWLEDGEMENTS

This book was written with the assistance of a grant from the Literature Board of the Australia Council for the Arts. I am extremely grateful for that support.

My thanks once more to Jane Palfreyman, Judith Lukin-Amundsen and Siobhán Cantrill for their editorial guidance, and to Donica Bettanin, Gayna Murphy, Andy Palmer, Renee Senogles and all at Allen & Unwin for helping this book reach its readers.

Thank you to Jane Johnson, Brian Murphy, Rebecca Hazel, Caroline Baum and David Roach for their help in various ways, and to my siblings and extended family for their loving support. Tegan Bennett Daylight, Eileen Naseby, Lucinda Holdforth, Vicki Hastrich and David Roach provided essential feedback on early drafts. It was invaluable, as was Michelle de Kretser's practical and moral support.

Among other books *Some We Love, Some We Hate, Some We Eat: Why It's So Hard to Think Straight About Animals* by Hal Herzog (HarperCollins, 2010), John Berger's *Why Look at Animals?* (Penguin, 2009) and *The Finlay Lloyd Book About Animals* (Finlay Lloyd, 2008) were useful and inspiring.

I'm especially grateful to Jenny Darling for her insight as a reader and professionalism as an agent, and to Jane Palfreyman for her tremendous publishing verve.

Sean McElvogue was a sensitive and insightful reader of various drafts, and has been steadfast in his support. He has my love and gratitude.

Charlotte Wood is the author of *The Children*, *The Submerged Cathedral* and *Pieces of a Girl*, *and* editor of *Brothers & Sisters*, an anthology of writing about siblings. Her novels have been shortlisted for various prizes, including the Australian Book Industry Awards, Miles Franklin Literary Award and the regional Commonwealth Writers' Prize.

Charlotte also writes the popular cookery blog How to Shuck an Oyster. *Love & Hunger*, her ode to good food, was published in 2012 to wide acclaim.

www.charlottewood.com.au